THE GALLERY

A REVERSE HAREM ROMANCE

MIKA LANE

HEADLANDS PUBLISHING

Copyright© 2018 by Mika Lane
Headlands Publishing
4200 Park Blvd. #244
Oakland, CA 94602

The Gallery is a work of fiction. Names, characters, (most) places, and incidents are either the product of the author's creativity or are used fictitiously. Any resemblance to actual persons, living or dead, events, or locales is entirely coincidental.
All rights reserved. This book or any portion thereof may not be reproduced or used in any manner whatsoever without the express written permission of the publisher except for the use of quotations in a book review.

BE THE FIRST TO KNOW...

Want more heat, heart,
and bad boys who know what they're doing?
Join my list and I'll send the steam straight to your inbox,
starting with a deliciously naughty story:

SIGN UP TO MY MAILING LIST!
Or visit:
https://geni.us/free-book-signup

1

____

AVRIL

THOSE GODDAMN HERMÈS BIRKIN BAGS WERE ALL OVER
the party.

I never understood the appeal of them—they were
these awful boxy things with strange angles, kind of
like a failed geometry test. And the cheapest ones
started at around ten grand. They, like the wrist-
watches everyone in my circle of acquaintances wore,
served as a sort of secret handshake. If you didn't have
one of each, well, then you weren't in the club.

I considered it the price of admission. And if you
truly belonged, you had an assortment to choose from,
depending on the day and your mood.

And yup, I had one. I'll admit it. I caved to the pressure. I might have preferred to carry one of those
thirty-dollar pleather jobs you can get at Target, but

hey, did I want these people to know about my humble beginnings? Half them probably couldn't even say where the Target store was (there were two—or was it now three?—in Manhattan).

People think that when you grow up and leave behind the confines of school and peer pressure, you're free. You can do whatever the hell you want. And maybe that's the way it is for some people.

But not for me.

The bullshit of growing up was just practice for *my* day-to-day existence.

If I wanted a life, friends, and to keep my marriage to one of the most successful men on Wall Street afloat, I had to be on top of my shit. I had to look the part, play the role, speak the language. It was really that simple.

But that didn't mean it was *easy*.

Interestingly, my husband of three years, Devon Crane, knew little of my past. I'd shared some, but not a lot, in order to satisfy any questions he, his family, or his business associates had. And fortunately, there weren't many questions—they'd seemed perfectly content with knowing I'd grown up in Baltimore, daughter of a local restaurateur, and not much more. It was a respectable and comfortable upbringing, they knew.

What they didn't know was that I had no complaints about my middle-class past, didn't feel underprivileged in the least, and had always enjoyed shopping at the humble Target. That additional information might have been a bit too much for them to process. Consequently, it never came up.

I kept that to myself, like a few other tidbits about my life.

So, it seemed the social pressures of growing up had turned out *not* to be something escapable, but in reality, one long warm-up practice for the world I married into. A world of aforementioned Hermès bags, private jets, limousines, and chic parties in the Hamptons.

But to tell the truth, as glam as it sounded, my lifestyle introduced pressures I'd never seen coming.

To deal with them, I kept my head down, figured out how to fit in, which was not hard if you spent enough money on enough of the right things, and tried to stop wondering why Devon Crane wanted to marry someone like me in the first place.

From where I stood on a terrace, just above a sprawling lawn overlooking the Atlantic Ocean, I watched people arriving at the fancy party. The crashing waves of the incoming tide drowned out the din of both conversation and the live music, making it look like people were moving their mouths without sound.

And my husband was nowhere to be found. Shit.

So I decided to look for him.

When I took my first step, my heel, my expensive spikey high heel, wedged between two brick pavers. The resulting jolt caused me to slosh gin and tonic out of my glass and all over my sister's watch, which I wore on my right wrist. *Dammit.*

I shook the cocktail off my arm and made sure the minute hand was still moving. If anything happened to that watch, well, I didn't know what I'd do. It was the only one I ever wore. Devon had insisted on gifting me a variety of much fancier ones in the time since we'd been married, and even one with diamonds for my thirtieth birthday, but I wasn't about to stop wearing Lisette's.

It was all I had left of her.

I recovered my balance and continued walking down the uneven (because, of course) brick steps leading to another tier of bars and catering and very thin, very well-dressed people. Still no Devon.

When my purse vibrated with the buzz of my phone, it was just a call from my assistant, Dagney. I let it go to voicemail. I could catch up with her later. Whatever it was, I trusted her to handle like the pro she was.

"Can I bring you another drink, miss?" a pony-tailed server asked. She must have witnessed my fumble because she handed me a napkin and relieved me of my nearly empty glass.

"Thank you," I said to the pretty young woman, who hurried off for the bar.

When I was re-loaded with a new beverage, I spotted a gaggle of women I knew from the charity circuit. I made my way toward them, this time being careful about where I stepped, and keeping my drink far from Lisette's watch.

As I got nearer, the ladies, decked out in their best Hamptons casual-chic, turned in my direction.

The odd thing was, though, that none returned my wave or smile. They just turned back to their huddle, inching more tightly together like a little pack of animals trying to keep warm. But it was too early in the season for any Fall crispness. In fact, we were nearly all wearing sleeveless dresses, and naturally, very expensive sunscreen.

But what really seemed off was that as I wove through the party, I spotted a couple other people, really just acquaintances, who also looked away from me. Was there something wrong with my dress? Had a bird crapped in my hair?

I scooted over to the edge of the patio as nonchalantly as possible and pretended to admire the crashing waves and seagulls dive-bombing the surf. I ran my hand through my hair. All clear there. I looked down at my dress, which was also flawless. Nothing but one tiny wrinkle, caused by the limo's seatbelt.

Okay. Let's try again.

"Hi everyone," I said with a giant smile, approaching the crowd of tightly packed women.

"Oh, hi, Avril. Great to see you," one of them said. The others just looked at each other, taking tiny sips of their drinks and holding their Birkin bags closer.

What the hell? We'd been in one of our charity

meetings only a couple days before. Everything had seemed normal then.

"Great to see you, too," I squeezed out with forced cheer. Something was off. I could smell it. Socializing with this crowd followed a strict set of rules. One tiny whiff of variance in peoples' behavior, and you knew something was up.

And it seemed that something had to do with me.

When it became clear no one else had a single thing to say, I knew to cut bait. "Well, I'm going to keep wandering. Hey, if any of you see my husband Devon, can you tell him I'm looking for him?"

Someone half-laughed, half-coughed. Okay, something was definitely up. And these bitches were not sharing a thing.

"Bye, Avril," one of them called as I walked away.

I waved over my shoulder without turning. Fuck them. I might live in their world now, but that doesn't mean I'd left Baltimore completely behind. I had enough smarts to be a bitch, too, when it was needed.

Nodding at a few other familiar faces, I made my way to a bench away from the crowd. First, I returned Dagney's call.

"Hey, Dagney." She was a godsend of an assistant, probably better at running my art gallery than I was. I'd be completely lost without her.

"Avril! Hi. Was just calling to let you know that new artist you wanted decided to sign with us. We can schedule his show next time you're in the gallery. I'm so excited."

Yes. I was, too.

"That is amazing. Great work. I'm out in the Hamptons at a party, waiting for Devon."

"Really? Have fun. I'm just finishing some things up," she said.

I'd been hoping to pull in the city's hottest surrealist painter, and it looked like my convincing had worked. My gallery was lucky enough to have a solid track record of signing some of the brightest new artists around, and selling the shit out of their work. It gave me no small satisfaction to beat out the more established galleries in the city.

Brokering art was a tough business, and I was a long way from being profitable. But luckily, my husband was supportive of my passion and was always ready with his checkbook, prepared to cover any of the gallery's losses.

Some people would call mine a *hobby job,* but I wasn't dabbling. I was seriously committed to building a real business.

Speaking of which, I dialed Devon again. No answer. He was probably at the party already, wandering around, looking for me.

He just couldn't hear his phone ringing.

Right?

2

SUMNER

"Yo, Sum," my business partners called from across the crazy-big lawn of one of the most crazy-big homes in the Hamptons.

The party was an extravagant one, as they tended to be in those parts. A birthday party for someone whose name I couldn't remember. It wasn't going to be any kind of crazy blowout or go late into the night, but it *was* the kind of party you wanted to both be invited to and show up to.

Everyone was there.

"Smith, Ash, how you assholes doing?" I said to the guys.

We'd all been together since our college days when we were broke and hungry, along with Chase and Gio who hadn't yet arrived. All that we'd accomplished since was nothing short of miraculous. 'Course, the people at the party who thought they knew me didn't know the half of it.

Which was fine.

"Dude, I have some Macallan coming our way with that hot-as-shit waitress over yonder. We've got some stuff to celebrate, boys," Smith said, pointing at a lovely young lady with a bouncy ponytail.

"Cheers to that," I said, grabbing one of the scotches off the pretty waitress's tray. I followed her ass, packed into some tight black pants, as she walked away.

An elbow collided with my ribs. "Hey, hey. Earth to Sumner."

"Sorry, guys. Just enjoying the… scenery."

They laughed.

I looked around the party. These Hamptons scenes always reminded me of something out of *The Great Gatsby*. Beautiful homes, beautiful people, beautiful views. Tragedy lurking in every secret. But I had to admit, I'd live here if it wasn't so fucking far from Manhattan.

"Okay, guys." Ash, our finance guy, cleared his throat and held up a glass to toast.

Smith and I looked at each other and rolled our eyes.

I glanced at my watch. "Ash, you have exactly thirty seconds to make your speech."

He dropped his arm in frustration and sloshed half

of his expensive drink onto the grass. "Fuck you, Sum. And fuck you, too," he said, looking at Smith.

"Sorry, Ash. It's just that we know how you go on, and on, and on… " I said.

"… and on, and on, and on," Smith added.

Ash furrowed his brow, his dark brown cheeks exhibiting a momentary pink hue.

"Ash, dude. Relax. We're just giving you a hard time," I said. "Hey, there's Chase and Gio," I said, waving across the lawn at our fourth and fifth business associates.

Ash rolled his eyes and waited for the other guys to join us before he raised his glass back into the air.

"I just want to say that, boys, we nailed it again. Another perfect acquisition for Roman, Edwards, Singh, Larlaith, and Rosselli. Cheers."

Yeah, it was a long-ass company name, so we usually went by our acronym *RESLR* which, when you said it out loud, sounded like *wrestler*. I thought it was idiotic to arrange our names to achieve that effect, but the other guys thought it was badass.

I took a deep draw on my scotch. Goddamn, the Macallan was amazing.

"We are gonna make some *money* off this baby," Smith added.

"Yup, we will at that," I said.

Although, I pretty much already had more money than I could ever hope to spend. But that wasn't why we did it, deals like this. It was for the thrill of it. Search and destroy, we joked.

"It is kind of a bummer about the airline mechanics who'll be losing their jobs," I said.

Ash looked down and shook his head. "Yeah, that part blows," he agreed. "Hopefully they'll get new ones."

I wasn't convinced. We'd bought a firm that contracted airplane maintenance to the airlines and with our new model and the contracts we'd designed, we had eliminated fifty percent of the workforce. Good for the company—not so much for the workers.

I hated that part of our business. We all did, actually.

The guys continued toasting and slapping each other on the back, anyway. In spite of the party being a daytime gathering, the alcohol was really flowing. Luckily, none of us had to drive back to the city. Our drivers would be handling that for us.

I excused myself for the men's room, but was only halfway there when another group of movers and shakers stopped me.

"Sumner!" I was offered several high-fives. "Heard about your latest victory. Congrats, brother."

Various other ambitious, successful guys chimed in.

"Thanks, thanks. Yeah, we're really pleased with how it all worked out," I said, nodding.

Those mechanics would find other jobs.

Right?

"Dude, it is true your dad's a U.S. Senator?" one of them blurted out.

Shit. I hated this question. It came up every now and again—always too often for my liking. Yeah, my dad was a U.S. Senator. He was also a fucking asshole.

"Yup, he's retiring this year, though," I said, nodding and hoping that would be the end of it.

But it wasn't. It never was.

My interrogator continued, "That is so cool. Have you ever met a president?"

Oh, for Christ's sake.

"No, I have not. My mom raised me. I barely ever saw my dad."

A couple of the guys in the group nodded. Most people knew my family story and were smart enough to talk about it behind my back instead of to my face.

That's the way things worked around there.

One of the guys nudged my questioner, who looked surprised, shrugged, and shut his trap.

"Hey, there she is," someone said, pointing.

Everyone turned toward a woman with long black hair, sitting alone on a bench, tapping away at her phone screen. I realized I knew her from somewhere when she looked up long enough to catch us checking her out.

Busted.

"Is that Avril Crane, wife of Devon Crane?" the nosy bastard asked.

"Well, she's his wife at the *moment*," someone snickered.

Christ, another one of *those* stories. They never ended with this crowd. I continued my walk toward the rest room, the conversation behind me fading.

"… wait 'til she finds out… "

"… she's a hottie, I'll take her out… "

"… that Devon sure is an asshole. She's better off without him… "

My phone vibrated in my pocket.

"Hey, Mom," I said, moving away from the crowd for privacy.

"Hi, sweetie, how are things?" she asked.

I decided not to tell her about the mention of my father.

"Good, Mom. What's up with you?"

"Well, I wanted to remind you I'm leaving for that Elder Hostel trip tomorrow. You know, the one where we go to Italy and help out with an archeological dig?"

I ran my hand through my hair. "Geez, Mom, I'm glad you called to remind me. I'd completely forgotten. That sounds amazing. Is it with the usual gang?"

I could hear her smiling. "It's with my usual gang, yes. Or *posse*, as you would call it. I'm rooming with Peggy, like I always do."

I looked up at the sky. I wouldn't have minded getting the hell out of town and spending some time in Italy, myself. The team's last deal had been a killer. Not friendly, and not nice.

"Mom, you have a great time. Do you have enough money? I can wire you some, just let me know, okay?"

"Oh, sweetie."

I heard the lump catch in her throat.

"You've already been so generous. I think I'm all set."

I loved nothing more than treating my mom. That woman had been to hell and back.

"Okay. Well don't hesitate to use your credit card. Buy yourself something nice, okay?"

"Love you, sweetie."

"Bye, Mom." She'd been my rock ever since my dad deserted us, and one of the high points of my life was spoiling her whenever she'd let me.

I knew what it was like to be left with nothing. That's why I worried about the airplane mechanics whose jobs we'd just obliterated.

3

AVRIL

"Miss, can I get you anything?"

The waitress from earlier happened by while I was trying to call Devon. So I requested another gin and tonic.

To avoid looking like a total wallflower, I took my drink and meandered over to the food. There was a magnificent spread of *hors d'oeuvres*, which included tiny oysters, stuffed squash blossoms, and something that looked like crab.

No one was eating any of it.

No one ever ate at these things. It was all just for show.

I still hadn't found my husband, but I wasn't sweating it. He'd eventually show up. He'd probably planned something special, seeing as our anniversary was next week, and had gotten tied up with that.

I couldn't wait to get my hands on the amazing necklace I was not supposed to know anything about.

I'd found it in the pocket of a jacket he'd left on the back of the sofa. I picked up after him whenever I could. There was so little housework to do because of all our staff, and I kind of missed the opportunity to nest, as my sister used to call it.

His gifts were always so generous.

He'd begun to woo me, just three and a half years ago, at the art gallery where I worked. On our third date, he gave me small diamond studs.

At the time, I'd thought the gift was over the top extravagant and a little weird—I barely knew the guy—but my best friend Blu convinced me that it was actually a modest gift from someone of Devon's means.

After we married, he'd gotten me my own gallery.

But tonight, he was over an hour late to the party, and to be honest, did he really plan our anniversary stuff, anyway? I suspected such tasks were carried out by someone on his admin team, and that was fine.

When you're as busy as Devon, you pay people to help you with those things. And I hoped he paid them a lot. I knew what a bear he could be when the pressure was on.

I made a beeline across the terrace when I spotted some of Devon's business associates.

"Avril, so nice to see you," one of them said, looking me up and down. What was his name? Ed?

The others muttered their greetings.

"Thanks. Hey, I've been waiting for Devon. Anybody seen him? He's not answering his phone."

It was the damnedest thing, but they all just stood and looked at me. Jesus, was there something in my teeth? I glanced down at my dress again, just to make sure I wasn't exposing myself.

A couple of them cleared their throats, and they looked away.

Where they avoiding my eyes, or was I just paranoid?

"Okay, then. I'll let you get back to your conversation. Sorry I interrupted." I turned to walk away.

The damn party was turning into a disaster.

But I stopped when a hand landed on my arm. It was the man I'd thought was named Ed. He was short and stocky, wore penny loafers with no socks, and was the kind of guy who was probably called Flounder by his college fraternity.

As I turned to face him, he didn't remove his hand. Instead, he ran a finger down my bare arm, leaving me with the heebie jeebies.

What the hell did he want? I stepped away from his touch.

"Ed, right?" I asked. I'd be sure to tell Devon about him later. He hated when men hit on me, especially the ones he did business with.

"You're right, sweetie. You're right." He jiggled the ice cubes in his glass.

I'm *sweetie*, now?

"What can I do for you, Ed?"

This crowd was generally very polite, especially when one had the urge to slap someone across the face. I was nothing if not a good student.

"Well, Avril, since you're looking for your hubby, I thought I'd help you out," he said.

I studied his soft, pale face. What was his deal? Was he married? I couldn't remember.

"How so, Ed?" I asked. I looked over his shoulder, where all the other men were watching us.

What in god's name was going on?

"Look, Avril." He tapped a finger on his lips. "Hey, what kind of name is that, anyway?"

Was this jerk really asking me this?

"It's French for April," I told him.

His eyebrows raised. Ugh.

"Okay, French for April. I'm not sure whether you know this or not, but I've done a bit of business with your husband over the years."

Didn't all these people do business together, on some level?

"Um, I don't know any details, but yes, that sounds right? What about it, Ed?" I looked at my watch. Lisette's watch.

He looked back at the group he'd come from, as if to make sure they were watching.

"You know what? I think it's time for me to go." I turned, but his hand gripped my forearm, locking me in place.

"Wait, wait. I'm sorry," he said with a grin. "I don't mean to waste your time. I just need to talk to you."

"Me? You need to talk to me? Why?" I jerked my arm out of his grip as casually as I could. I didn't want to draw attention. That is, aside from his cronies who were already watching our show.

"Avril, I'm gonna do you a favor. Mainly because I think your husband is a goddamn, lying, cheating, fucker," Ed said.

Oh my god, did he really just say that?

My face was immediately on fire, and if I didn't sit down soon, I'd be in trouble.

"Um… what… ?" I sputtered. "Wh… what are you talking about?" I attempted to steady my voice. It didn't work too well.

He moved closer.

"Avril, please forgive my foul language. I can see you're a nice woman. But your husband is balling another woman. I probably wouldn't share this with you if I didn't think he was such a dick, one who deserved to suffer."

My gin and tonic thumped to the ground, the ice cubes rolling across the grass. I took a step back, and my skinny heel caught again.

This time, Ed caught me before I tumbled over.

"Hey, be careful. I know this is not easy to hear. But

I thought you should know." He reached into his pocket.

"Please feel free to pass my business card on to your husband so he knows where you got this important information." For a moment, the smug look on his face faded, replaced by compassion or pity. I wasn't sure which. "I'm sorry. I really am," he added.

Lightheaded, I climbed the brick stairs toward the house in what felt like slow motion, gripping the handrail as it if were my lifeline. My legs weren't going to carry me all on their own.

Devon? *Balling*? That meant having sex, screwing, fucking, right? A woman other than *me*, right? My Devon? We'd been married a happy three years. No issues. None at all. Barely any fights. We'd had sex just... well, shit, I couldn't remember.

Putting one foot in front of the other, I wove through the throngs of well-dressed people. Left, right, left, right. If I continued like that, I'd eventually get to the driveway in front of the house, where I could find my waiting limo and get the hell out of there. I turned back to see Ed and his gaggle of friends. They were deep in conversation with each other, with the exception of Ed, who was watching me walk away. If I wasn't mistaken, his doughy face looked a little sad.

I left behind the partygoers, there to see and be seen. And in Ed's case, to hurt, maim, destroy, and if possible, kill.

When I finally reached the house, I was stumbling

through it when a door flew open—I presume from a restroom—and the cute ponytailed waitress of earlier came rushing out, tucking in stray hairs. She looked embarrassed when I caught her eye, looked down, and dashed off. And wouldn't you know, right behind her was a tall, good-looking man with a strong brow and a dimple in the middle of his chin. His black hair was mussed, and he was tucking in his shirt. I knew him from somewhere...

Was everyone messing around—except for me?

"Oh. Hello," he said, stopping.

Had I just caught him in a hook-up?

"Hello..."

"Sumner. Sumner Larlaith. It's nice to see you." He extended his hand. "Avril, right?"

I was in no condition for small talk.

"Right. Hi, Sumner, good to see you again. Enjoy the party," I said, hustling for the door.

How did I know that guy?

I fumbled through my bag for my phone. I needed to call my driver. And while I was waiting—I don't know why—I dialed Devon's phone again, hoping against hope that Ed had been wrong, or just plain mean.

Or both.

4

CHASE

God, was I glad to be back home, and for having spent the night in my own bed. Manhattan was funny that way. Once you were hooked on it, you hated being away from it.

I mean, the Hamptons were great and all, but they weren't the *city*.

It had been another boring-ass Hampton's party with the guys—same people, same cocktails, same conversation. I wasn't sure why I did it to myself, going to these things, especially when I had something much more important waiting for me at home, except that the rest of my buddies thought it was really important. The two hours it took to get there and back really threw off my schedule. And yeah, it was good to hang with my business partners, but I spent too many of my waking hours with them, anyway.

However, when you're ambitious like we were, you had to be sure to keep your name and face in front of the people who mattered.

Even if, in a perfect world, they wouldn't normally give you the time of day, and vice versa.

I had an hour or so before I had to leave for the office that morning, so after my workout and shower, I pulled on some sweats and a T-shirt. I settled onto the sofa with some coffee and the *New York Post*, although I didn't count on being able to read much of the paper.

My eight-month-old, Ruby, would be stirring in her room, and the nanny would be bringing her out to me shortly. The highlight of my day, really, laying eyes on my beautiful daughter.

But until she was in my arms, I flipped to the page where my team and I had been interviewed about last week's business deal. I wanted to see what the *Post* had to say.

They placed us in a little section that usually featured the city's up-and-comers, complete with a crappy black and white photo of me and the guys. We did look like the young masters of the universe we fancied ourselves, which would make Smith, Ashera, and Gio very happy. Sumner could take or leave that sort of thing. He thought that stuff was pure vanity.

I'd always figured his perspective was the result of being a senator's son and always being in the spotlight

—or in his case, always on the edge of the spotlight. But I didn't ask. It was better not to.

I knew he'd been tweaked that someone at the party had asked him about his dad, U.S. Senator Victor Larlaith. I'd cringed when I overhead the conversation. The poor bastard couldn't seem to go a week without someone connecting the two of them and jumping to the conclusion that they were a real family.

I'd heard bits and pieces of the story about how the senator flat-out dumped Sumner and his mother, and yet, the questions about his father dogged him, each time re-opening a wound he probably would have liked to heal.

From what I'd heard, the man had left them for his secretary when Sum was small. Apparently, he'd paid only the bare minimum child support back then, which hadn't amounted to much because at the time he'd been managing a moderately successful car dealership in New Jersey.

He worked his way up the ranks in local politics, though, and ended up owning several dealerships before heading to Washington as a senator. The child support payments had increased, but his visits had not. Sum did tell me once that he'd gotten only one birthday card from his father in his whole life.

As the nanny placed Ruby in my arms, and I gazed down at her perfect little face, I couldn't imagine walking out on my kid. Ever.

Men did some fucked up things. But so did women.

Particularly Ruby's mother. She'd bailed when the baby was only two months old. Our relationship had been a rocky one, so it was no surprise that we split. And if she could walk out on her kid that easily, good riddance to her.

So I could really understand why Sum chafed when people put them together, and even more so when they assumed his success was owed to his being a senator's son.

Which it was not. He, like the rest of us, earned every goddamn penny we had with no help from anyone.

The happy buzz I'd earned from my workout had drifted away, but came flooding back as soon as my squirmy girl was in my arms. She smelled like fresh, clean baby, thanks to the nanny.

As I fed with her, I flicked on the TV to keep more news running in the background. I clicked channels and stopped on an image of the black-haired woman I'd seen at the Hamptons party—the one who'd been sitting alone, fiddling with her phone. If I remembered correctly, she didn't seem to be having much fun, and now I could see why.

Her husband was *the* Devon Crane, one of the biggest wheelers and dealers in Manhattan, and it seemed he'd just dumped her ass.

I didn't get why this was on cable news. After all, didn't couples break up all the time? But as the story continued, I learned he was also under investigation by

the district attorney for some sort of pyramid invest-
ment scheme.

Holy shit.

His wife, or ex, or whatever she should be called, was absolutely stunning, and for the few seconds she was on my TV screen, I couldn't move. Avril. That was her name. She had glorious long hair and big, dark eyes. Kind of exotic looking, actually.

I put on my earpiece while I continued feeding Ruby, and dialed my friend, Blu.

"What?" he said, yawning. "Why the hell are you calling me so early, Chase? Don't you know how important beauty sleep is to gay men?"

Eh. I didn't feel so badly. First, it was seven a.m., so not obscenely early, and second, it wasn't my fault Blu was a night owl.

"Blu, wake up. Seven a.m.'s not that early. Get your butt out of bed." He was one of my best friends from college, and every aspect of his life was high drama since he'd come out of the closet. As if we hadn't all known he was gay back then, anyway.

Over the phone, I heard something rustle. I knew what that meant.

"Chase," he said, as a door clicked in the back-ground. He continued in a low voice, "My date from last night is still over, and he's looking very cute, snoring ever so lightly, so you'd better make this fast. My morning missile is ready to go."

"Jesus, down boy. You act like you don't get laid every day of your life."

I'd have to clean up my language before Ruby started talking, the nanny constantly reminded me. Otherwise, I'd have a little cutie with a big, filthy mouth. Just like her papa.

"It's none of your business how often I get laid, although I could swear I hear some resentment coming out of that heterosexual mouth of yours. I've told you before, it's easier to get dick than pussy. You could always come play for my team." He snickered.

"Thanks, man. I appreciate the offer. It's really tempting."

He never gave up.

I suppressed a snicker. "Look, I'll make it quick so you can get back to your stud. Aren't you friends with the wife of Devon Crane?"

"You better fucking bet I am. Avril Crane is my best girl. If I wasn't a fag, I'd be getting in her pants."

"I'm sure she'd love to know that."

"She does know! I tell her all the time. Anyway, what about her?" he asked.

"I just saw on the news that she and her husband are splitting."

I no sooner had the words out and he screamed loudly enough to split my eardrum. I think the baby even heard it. Her eyes had popped wide open.

"*NO FUCKING WAY*. Oh my god oh my god oh my

god. I gotta call her. I'll talk to you later." And he was gone.

So much for his date.

I hadn't told him Crane was also under investigation, but I figured he'd hear that soon enough for himself.

I moved on to another call. It wouldn't be too early for the next guy. We were both early risers.

"Gio. How you doin' man?" I asked when he'd picked up.

He was just as chipper as Blu had been groggy.

Ruby had finished her bottle and was smacking her lips, all milky and delicious. I hated to do it, but I handed her over to the nanny. She'd bring her by my office later, so I could give her another bottle and play with her while I was wheeling and dealing.

One of the many advantages of being one of the bosses at work was that if I wanted to spend time my baby, you'd better goddamn believe I would do just that.

"*Buongiorno*, brother," Gio said.

He'd been away from Italy for a long time but would never stop trying to teach me, and the rest of the guys, his beautiful language. He'd been working on us since college, and all these years later, I was able to say about five words, which was more than the others could, put together.

"I know you're at the office already, but I was

hoping you could switch gears for a sec. What sort of shape are we in for tonight?" I asked.

Papers rustled in the background, and I heard tapping on a keyboard.

"Let's see. Here we go. We have about one hundred fifty guests for the party," he reported.

"Wow. That's good stuff." With that many people, we were at capacity, but we always made room for extra women if they really wanted in. It was the least we could do.

"Yes, it is. I'm going over to check out the venue one last time, and we'll be all set."

"Cool, thanks. It will be nice to kick back and relax tonight. I need it after that tight-assed party in the Hamptons."

Gio snickered. "Well, *amico*, those Hamptons folks are the very people making us extremely successful right now, so watch your disdain for them."

"I am, don't worry, I am. Who knew those prepster types were such a bunch of pervs?" I said, amused.

"Hey, you're one to talk."

And he was right. I said my goodbyes and got up to dress for work—my day job as a finance hot shot, and my night job as a sex party promoter for Manhattan's elite.

Guess which one I liked better?

5

AVRIL

"HOLY SHIT, GIRL. THAT IS SOME KIND OF STORY," BLU said, holding one of my hands while I blew my nose with the other.

I looked up at his kind eyes. Every woman should have a gay best friend. Especially an adorable one with red hair and freckles.

I nodded at him, only slightly uncomfortable with shedding a few tears at one of the city's top lunch spots. I was not, however, about to start sobbing into my chilled celery soup and gluten-free breadsticks.

Not that I'd eat the breadsticks. I didn't eat carbs.

"Worst of all, Blu," I said with a sniffle, "you know *who* he was fucking? You want to know who?"

Of course, he wanted to know. He wanted to know more than he wanted air to breathe or water to drink.

33

"Tell me, baby. Tell me who the nasty whore is," he begged.

"Dagney."

"Who?"

"Dagney. You know her." The sobs were dangerously close. I might have to excuse myself for the ladies' room.

"DAGNEY?" he screamed.

I looked around the room as the glances shot our way. *Nothing to see here, folks. Please get back to your lunches.*

I lowered my voice for privacy, hoping Blu would follow with his inside voice. "Yup."

"Get out. Dagney, your assistant? That little thing with the curly hair and glasses?"

I pressed a tissue against my mouth in case a wail were to try and escape. Because of that, I couldn't speak.

So I just nodded.

"Holy. Shit."

I nodded some more.

"That nasty, fucking bitch. You gave her a job and taught her everything she knows."

I kept nodding, although I couldn't really see Blu now.

The tears were fully blurring my vision, and it was all I could do to keep up with my runny nose. I wouldn't be eating a thing for lunch, which kind of bummed me out. I really loved celery soup.

And Blu was right. I'd taken Dagney under my wing. She'd been a recent art history grad with no prospects—I mean, what prospects does any art history major have?—and I taught her everything I knew about running a gallery.

My gallery, I might add, which was known as one of fastest "up and comers" in all of Manhattan.

So now, I was down one husband. And one assistant.

It wasn't fucking fair.

My distress was obvious, and not going to subside anytime soon, so Blu waved at the waitress for the check. I must have really looked bad because if Blu glances around the room to see if people are looking, they most definitely are.

"Don't worry, sweetie, we're getting you out of here."

I fished through my Birkin bag and placed my AmEx on the table. I figured I'd charge everything to Devon for as long as I could.

But it turned out that wasn't to be for long. The waitress returned with a smug face.

"Ms. um, Crane. Your card didn't go through." She took a step back when she realized the shape I was in.

I fished for another card. I never let Blu pay. After all, I was the one who'd landed a loaded husband.

But that card didn't go through either.

"Oh, for chrissakes, here take my card," he said, thrusting his Visa at the waitress.

He could afford one lunch. He did quite well for himself with some party-planning business he had.

"My cards…my cards…" was all I could mumble. Why weren't my credit cards working?

BLU and I walked over to the closest branch of my bank, my arm hooked through his like I was a feeble old lady. The greeter saw the shape I was in and immediately brought us to a small cubicle in a corner, affording me a modicum of privacy.

"Our manager will be right with you," she said, backing away slowly.

Blu nodded, and put an arm around me. "Thank you," he said to her. He was good in a crisis, as long as it wasn't *his* crisis.

About five minutes later, a very serious branch manager settled into his desk and looked from me to Blu and back. His mouth pressed into a hard, thin line, and he folded his hands in front of him.

He spoke very slowly. "Has someone important passed away?"

We both looked at him in silence, but Blu came to his senses first.

"My friend here, Avril Crane—sweetie, can you give the man your picture ID?—just had her credit cards refused at lunch. Can you tell us if everything's okay with her accounts?"

The manager looked at my driver license, and back to me. I guess I was pretty unrecognizable with mascara pooling under my eyes and a tissue constantly under my nose.

"Is there a reason everything might not be okay with your accounts, Ms. Crane?" he asked.

I nodded, but my chest was in convulsions from all the crying, and I still couldn't speak. I gestured for Blu to explain.

"She's um... well, there are some problems at home," Blu said with a nod and a wink, to emphasize the gravity of his euphemism.

And the bank manager understood loud and clear. He jumped to his feet with my ID in hand. The shit they must hear about...

"I see. I'll be right back. Don't worry, Ms. Crane. We'll get this figured out." He dashed off, shaking his head.

While the bank manager was doing whatever bank managers did, Blu took the opportunity to make me feel worse than I already did, if that were possible.

"So, have you heard from him? I mean, did he tell you to your face?"

I sniffled loudly. It seemed as if the tears were subsiding, at least for a momentary break.

I cleared my throat. "I got home from that party in

the Hamptons, after trying to call him the entire time. He never once picked up."

Blu thoughtfully reached into my bag for another tissue, after taking the snotty ones from my hand and throwing them in the waste bin. That's a true friend for you.

"So, I couldn't get ahold of him. When I got home, there was a note, and his closet was cleaned out. The whole thing seemed like a joke. A bad joke."

The tears threatened again.

"What did the note say?"

"That basically he was out of there, he was sorry, and that he'd fallen in love with another woman. Oh, and that he'd always love me, too. He said I could have his stereo."

Blu's eyes were huge, and his mouth was opened to a small circle. He reminded me of a hungry baby bird.

"His *stereo*? You know, I never really liked him…" he started to say, shuddering from the indignation.

I put my hand up.

"People always say that *after* the fact. It's not doing me a bit of good right now."

"Sorry, sweetie. Just trying to help. Anyway, how'd you find out it was Dagney?"

"I put two and two together. First, she left me a note at the gallery that she was resigning. She'd thrown her key back through the mail slot after she left."

I had to say, she did a good job of finishing up everything she'd been working on. She was conscientious that way. Didn't do anything halfway, including steal my husband.

"Okay, so she quit. How did that give it away?" Blu asked.

"Well, I was outside the gallery, locking up to go home, and the owner of the gallery across the street came over to tell me she'd seen Dagney's *husband* spending a lot of time in the gallery, especially at night, after closing time."

"But Dagney has no husband, right?"

"Exactly," I said.

Where had where the damn bank manager had gone?

"I asked her to describe the man, and boom. It was my Devon."

"*What?*" Blu gasped. "Jesus Christ. You can't make this shit up."

We turned toward some rustling papers and found the manager standing right there.

"I'm sorry to interrupt, but I have some information for you." His tone was low and quiet. I guess it sort of *was* as if someone died. He settled back into his chair, and Blu tossed the rest of my soggy tissues.

"Ms. Crane, it seems as if all but one of your joint accounts with... " he flipped through some papers, "... here we are, Mr. Devon Crane, have been closed. There is one that remains open, with a balance of... " He slipped a piece of paper that looked like a cash register receipt across the desk towards me.

Blu grabbed it before I could see it. *"What the fucking fuck?"* he screamed, standing and shaking the piece of paper. He leaned over the desk toward the manager, who'd moved back in terror.

But Blu wasn't letting him off the hook. "Please check again. It's not possible my friend here has an account with a balance of only"—he clutched the piece of paper to his chest as if his heart were breaking, then lowered his voice to a whisper—"one thousand freaking dollars. You know how loaded her husband is?"

Holy fucking shit. I go from a Park Avenue penthouse and a limo to take me everywhere to a bank account with one thousand dollars? Actually, he'd not taken away the penthouse or the limo. Yet.

Tears didn't threaten this time. A nauseous stomach did.

Blu took returned to his seat and the bank manager recovered, leaning toward me. "Ms. Crane, you have a job, right?"

I nodded, wondering where he was going. I didn't know if I should go as far as explaining that it was more of a sort-of job. Like, I didn't really make any money at it.

He snapped back in his chair.

"Okay. I think all will be well then," he said with a proud smile, like he'd just discovered a cure for cancer.

Maybe that was why people hated banks.

Yeah, I had the gallery, and yes, it was growing

nicely. But after covering some very expensive rent, catering for openings, and the generous salary I paid my ex-assistant Dagney the whore, there wasn't much left. I didn't even pay myself. I donated any extra money we had to the school down the street, the Children's Art Center, where I volunteered.

Devon had liked calling these activities my hobbies. Fucker.

Shit. Speaking of volunteering, I had to be downtown in forty-five minutes for the drawing lesson I was scheduled to teach. I stood, leaving the bank manager and Blu discussing my financial situation.

"Oh, honey, you think you're up for teaching, today?" Blu asked, taking my hand to pull me back to my seat. Evidently, he wasn't done with my suffering.

But I was, at least for the moment. "Yeah. Yeah, I am," I said, smoothing out my dress. "I gotta go." I shook the bank manager's hand.

His face brightened when he realized we were leaving.

Outside in the blinding sunshine, I pulled on my designer sunglasses while my limo zipped up to the curb. Devon hadn't thought to take that away.

At least not yet.

6

<hr>

GIO

With a long day and night ahead of me, I sucked down an afternoon cup of *caffè* at the office while I scrolled through my online calendar.

My schedule was booked so solid that day, I didn't know when I'd be able to relieve myself, and the guys kept pinging me about the night's upcoming party, since I was the one to handle the venue arrangements.

Why couldn't I get a break?

I had to admit, though, I wouldn't have it any other way. I buzzed our admin.

"Is our next meeting here?"

"They just arrived, Gio. I put them in the big conference room and let the others know."

I'd worked for months to set up a meeting with some of the city's most successful private equity firms to see if they wanted to throw some money at our ventures. I took my place at the head of the conference room table after a round of hellos and introductions.

"I'm Gio Rosselli, one of the founding partners of RESLR. Thank you all for attending."

Some of the faces looked familiar, and others were new. I coasted through my presentation with a particular emphasis on our latest acquisition, the airline mechanic company. Just as I was wrapping up, a hand went up in the back of the room. I pointed, and the man stood.

"Gio, I'm Devon Crane from Crane Enterprises. I think what you're offering could be a good fit with our business objectives..."

He kept talking, but I was having trouble following him.

Devon Crane...how did I know that name?

Oh shit, that was the guy who was in the news the other day. The scumbag who'd dumped his wife *and* who was under investigation.

I wanted nothing to do with this guy.

As everyone filtered out of the room after the meeting ended, I caught up with him.

"Devon, thank you again for joining the meeting," I said, extending my hand for a shake.

He beamed. "Thank you, Gio. I think we could really make some things happen together."

Yeah, like enjoy prison food? I wouldn't have done business with that *cretino* if my life depended on it. But

I wore my smile like a shield and turned to shake the hand of the pretty associate he'd brought along.

"Where are my manners?" Devon asked with a laugh. "This is my fiancée, Dagney Gardner."

Fiancée? The man was still married. And as if he didn't already look sleazy enough, he dug himself in even deeper.

"Yeah, Gio," he said, putting an arm around my shoulder like we were old buddies.

I was dying to shake him off, but wanted to hear what he had to say.

He turned me slightly toward the wall for privacy.

"You see, it's time for some new ventures for me and my firm. I just got out of a bad, bad marriage. You know how it is. The woman was a loon." He did the twirling crazy finger thing next to his head for emphasis. "My new woman, Dagney, *gets* me. She wants to learn my business. She wants to be by my side."

Was he fucking kidding?

No, no, no. I backed up a step. "Well, my friend, I really don't want to know about your relationships, and I think it's pretty shitty to even bring them up during a business meeting. Further, you are under investigation by the D.A., so you have a lot of nerve showing up here."

"Well…but… " he sputtered.

"Sorry, my friend. We won't be doing any business together, and I'd appreciate if you left my office right now."

His face turned deep red. He grabbed his fiancée's hand, and they marched out of the office.

Smith and Ash caught me in the hallway.

"What was that all about?" Ash asked me.

I shook my head. "You know what an asshole that man is, right? There's no way we're doing business with him."

Ash looked around to make sure all our guests had left the office. "Gio, I appreciate your concern, but isn't that the kind of decision we usually make together, after some analysis and discussion?"

I didn't need any egalitarian *merda* right then.

I ran my hand through my hair, frustration levels rising.

"Look guys, sorry. I just think there are some scum-bags out there we don't need to be affiliated with. Google the latest on Devon Crane. You'll see."

I'D HAD ENOUGH for one day. At least of my day job, that was for sure. I headed over to the venue for the evening's party to see how the set up was going.

Chase and Blu were directing people with last minute preparations.

"Things are looking good, guys," I said to Blu, who began unpacking a giant box of condoms.

I glanced around the huge loft space we'd managed

to lease for the last time. The building was being turned into condos, so we were on the lookout for someplace new.

"Can I see the guest list?" I asked Chase. That was his area to handle.

"Sure, Gio. Here ya go," he said, passing me an iPad.

While a lot of our attendees RSVP'd with their fake "club" names, I saw several familiar ones—people who'd been attending Kink Lab consistently in the two years since we'd started it.

There were other sex parties in New York. The city was freaking full of them, like every major metropolitan area. You just had to find out about them, which was not hard because people had big fucking mouths. But Kink Lab was different.

You had to be invited, which meant a current member had to vouch for you, and then you had to be vetted. If you were granted membership, you then had to pay not only a steep membership fee but also a high admission charge for each party attended. But it was worth it, and I knew tonight's event would be another huge success.

"Hey Gio, I gotta run home and make sure the babysitter is all set up. I'll be back in an hour or so," Chase said.

"Sounds good. I'm just going to chill out, have a drink, and try to forget my day." I went behind the bar that had just been set up for the party and poured myself a nice, dark beer. "By the way, how is your *bambina*?"

Chase's face lit up. It had been only a few months since his ballet dancer girlfriend had said *arrivederci*, leaving him with their little Ruby, and he was doing a great job on his own. I had to hand it to him.

"Princess Ruby is great. Getting fatter every day." He shook his head.

I'd never seen him as happy as he'd been since Ruby had come along.

"And you know, Gio, I wouldn't have it any other way."

"I know it. You're killing the fatherhood thing. Wish I'd had a *papa* like you." Chase was one of the few who knew my story—and why my family had to flee Italy years ago.

"See you in an hour, man," he said.

I watched the bubbles rise in my beer glass as I enjoyed the first quiet moment I'd had in a while to mull over the events of the day.

Damn if that Crane guy wasn't a huge dickhead. Seriously, who comes to a meeting to drum up new business when they're under investigation by the D.A. *and* brings their new girlfriend, particularly when he's only left his wife days before?

Who fucking does that?

Sumner clapped me on the back, snapping me out of my reverie. "You look lost in thought, brother."

I stretched my neck and rolled my shoulders. "*Si.*

It's been a strange day. You know that financier, Devon Crane, from our meeting today? Had the nerve to refer to the wife he'd left just a week ago as a 'nutbag.'"

"The world is full of people who are not very *simpatico*. I think you know that as well as anyone," Sumner said.

I loved it when my friends used the Italian words I was always trying to teach them.

And yup, I did know as well as anyone about the creeps of the world. All I had to do was take a look at my arms-dealer father and how he'd thought nothing of putting our entire family in danger.

And I was curious to know if that woman we'd seen at the Hampton's party really was as nutty as her husband said.

If Crane was as full of shit as I knew he was, *he* was the nut for leaving *her*.

7

AVRIL

AT FOUR FIFTY-FIVE P.M., I LOCKED THE GALLERY DOOR, placed the *be right back* sign in the window, and returned to my office.

At exactly five p.m., the phone rang.

"Devon," I said, stomach churning.

"Av," he replied.

I was swirling in a volcano of emotions, ratcheting back and forth between sadness, humiliation, and downright hatred. I moved my office trashcan between my legs in case I needed to vomit.

I forced myself to remain calm and cool. He wasn't going to get the satisfaction of my freaking out.

"I was glad to get your email. Thank you for suggesting we speak," I said.

"I figured it was about time. You know I'm with Dagney now, don't you?"

A knife in my chest would have been less painful.

I held my chin high, even though nobody could see it. "I know that. I figured it out, Devon."

"Oh. I wasn't sure you knew."

"Yup. I know," I said simply.

If he was waiting for me to yell at him, he would be waiting a long time.

"Devon?" I asked.

"Yes, Avril?"

"Is there a reason you cut off the credit cards and emptied our joint bank accounts? I mean, do you think that's fair, after you left me with no warning?"

Okay, now my blood was starting to boil. I flicked on my laptop and looked at pictures of kittens.

"Well, Av, don't you think it's time you started…you know, supporting yourself?"

Stay calm. "If that's your feeling, we could have talked about it. There might have been better ways to communicate that than just cutting me off without warning."

"You're right. You're right. It's just that all the guys I know said to be careful, and that when you got the news, you'd try to clean me out."

"Glad to know your guy friends, who were probably also *my* friends at one time, advised you to leave me penniless," I said.

"Oh, come on, Avril, it's not like that—"

"It is exactly like that, Devon. The minute you turned your back on me, most of our friends did, too. And you know why that is?" I was getting pissed now.

"Um…well…I didn't know that—"

"It's because you have the money, Devon. Plain and simple. It's not because they like you better. They like your *money* better."

"Oh, I don't know about that…look, you're going to have to get a real job. No more fun at the gallery."

He did not just say that, did he?

"Devon, we were married three years. We were in love. At least, I loved you. And now this. I don't understand it. The courts are going to demand that you pay me, so why don't you start now?"

"There! I knew you were a gold digger," he said. "And the limo is going away. You're going to have to start taking the subway. Or even driving. Get a car." This made him cackle.

And he knew that one particular threat would hurt me like no other.

"Devon, I can't believe you would bring that up…"

"Oh, really? Well, let me tell you something. You haven't gotten behind the wheel of a car since your sister—"

A buzzing sounded in my ears, increasing in volume. It was accompanied by white dots in front of my eyes.

"—but I think it's high time you got over that and started driving again."

I'd never heard his voice so cruel.

Oh, god. He hit the one spot in my heart that crippled me. My hand shook so violently that when I went to swipe my phone closed, it flipped out of my hand and skittered across the desk and onto the floor.

The buzzing and white lights exploded in my head, and I grabbed my office trashcan just in time to be sick. My shoulders shook from convulsions, following by a heaving in my chest.

The sobs came again, and this time, it seemed like they'd never stop.

I LIFTED my head toward a rattling at the gallery's front door and pushed myself up from my chair. I lumbered across the room like I'd been run over by a truck.

"Av, let me in!" Blu's muffled voice shouted.

I unlocked the door, and he slipped inside, locking it behind himself.

"Baby, I'm so glad you called me." He grabbed my arms and led me back to the office.

I was no longer crying, but I couldn't stop shaking.

"Are you cold, sweetie? Here, put this shawl around your shoulders. I'm gonna make some tea. You want some tea?"

"Yeah."

"So what happened?" he asked, after he'd put the kettle on.

Thank god for gay boyfriends. I already felt tons better just having him there. And his turquoise bow tie was just perfect with his red hair.

"Well, it was the first time we'd spoken since he left. He brought up my sister, just to be mean. Threw it all right in my face."

"Oh, that bastard! I'm so sorry." He was one of the few who knew the story of Lisette.

I sipped my tea.

"I know. It just threw me for a loop. Especially the way he said it. It was so vicious. Actually, beyond vicious. I had no idea I was married to such a brutal man. God, I feel so stupid."

"You know, sweetie, people surprise me every day." Blu waved a hand in the air. "That's all I can say. Now, how 'bout we get you up and get a little dinner in your belly?"

"Thank god I have you, Blu."

"Don't thank me. I'm sure I'll be crying on your shoulder one of these days, myself."

He bundled me into my light Fall coat, and we walked under the streetlights to the little Italian joint on the corner.

THREE GLASSES of wine and a giant plate of pasta later, and I was feeling much better. What a fool I'd been, avoiding carbs all that time.

Blu leaned across the table. "I may have a solution to your financial situation. At least temporarily. It could help you with your cash flow."

My heart jumped. If I had to give up the gallery along with my marriage, well, that would be way more than I could take.

"Seriously? What are you thinking?"

You never knew what Blu had up his sleeve. He was a wheeler and dealer of epic proportions.

"So." He lowered his voice and glanced around. "You know how I'm involved with party promotions?"

"Yeah. What about it?" I took huge mouthful of pasta. I didn't usually take huge mouthfuls of anything, but after that day, I felt entitled.

I'd watched my weight so carefully over the years, I'd forgotten what pasta even tasted like. Fuck those skinny, Birkin-carrying bitches.

Pasta was *good*.

"The parties I promote are *sex* parties, Av." He stared at me like he was waiting for my head to explode.

I shrugged "I thought it was something like that. You know, part of your gay secret life you never tell me about."

"You kidding?" he said with a huff. "All along, you

thought I was up to something…shall we say *unconventional*…and you never said anything?"

Was he offended I'd not called him out? I figured he'd tell me if and when he wanted to.

"I respect your privacy, Blu. Didn't want to pry. I know the gay community has a different way of mixing and mingling."

Did I just say that? I sounded like someone's grandma, leaving Blue with a funny look on his face. One I'd not seen before.

"Yeah, well, the parties I'm talking about are a bit different than what you thought."

"What do you mean?" I asked.

Not sure I wanted to hear about them, but on the other hand, I was morbidly curious.

"They're not the gay parties you think they are."

Oh. "What are they then? I mean, are you into kiddie porn? Please say no, Blu."

"Av! Give me a fucking break. That's gross. The parties are not *gay*. They're straight."

I laughed. "What are you doing at a straight sex party, for god's sake?"

"I *organize* them. I don't have sex at them. I have a team of guys I work with, and we host them for the city's elite. Very exclusive. Very expensive."

"Why aren't you running gay parties?" I asked.

"You're still stuck on that?" He rolled his eyes. "Because there are tons of gay sex parties. The money is in the straight parties. There aren't as many of them, and the really nice ones are hard to come by. And we can charge a shitload for them."

Geez. A whole world out there I was unaware of.

"Okay. So how does this involve me and my pathetic money situation?"

"Well, Av," he said. "What would you say to using the gallery for a party or two? We're needing a new location. It could be very lucrative for you."

The waiter brought two tiramisu. One for each of us. My days of having one little bite of someone else's dessert were *over*.

"Oh, c'mon. I can't have a sex party at my gallery," I laughed. God, that was some good tiramisu. It was all I could do to not moan out loud.

"No? Why not?" he asked. "The place sits empty six nights out of the week. Or more."

"What if something gets damaged?"

"It's a sex party, not a keg party. We have security, and anyone who gets out of hand is sent on their way. And we have a cleaning crew come in afterwards. They put all our furniture back in storage until the next party."

He was serious. Unbelievable.

"What do you mean, furniture?"

"Well, what do you think the people fuck on? The cold, hard floor?" He rolled his eyes so hard, I wondered how they didn't pop out of his head.

He could be awfully touchy.

"Well, I don't know. I hadn't thought about it. I

mean, do you bring in a dozen beds or something? How would I know what people fuck on at sex parties?" Now *I* was getting pissy.

A few heads turned our way. Shit.

He rolled his eyes again. Apparently, he'd had no idea that I, his best friend, was such a total dumbass. He sighed deeply, pushed to the brink of his patience.

He spoke very slowly and quietly, as if lecturing a naughty little kid. "We bring in cushy sofas and tufted mattresses. The finished look is kind of bohemian and harem-ish, with floaty fabrics, rugs, sumptuous materials, giant floor cushions. That sort of thing."

I guess if I were going to a sex party, I'd want it to be kind of nice.

Now, it was my turn to lower my voice. "And are people just having sex...everywhere? Like a giant orgy?" While it all sounded awfully bizarre, thinking about it left me... Well, never mind. I didn't need to be thinking of things like that when I'd probably never be having sex again.

"No! People come in with partners, or women come alone—men can't come in by themselves, they must have a date—some people keep to themselves, and some hook up with others. It's really whatever you want, so long as it's all consensual."

"Can you just hang out and watch?" I had to admit, and maybe it was from the wine I'd just drunk, that something about having sex in public sounded kind of hot.

Blu called the waiter over and ordered after-dinner drinks. I'd have to fast for days after this meal to fit into my wardrobe. The skinny bitches in Pilates called them their *hungry days*. Like a wrestling team, they'd starve themselves until they made weight.

"Yeah, you can watch as long as you're not creepy about it. Anyway, what do you say? You could make a lot of money letting us use your space."

His face lit up in with a hopeful smile, revealing the gap between his teeth that I loved so much. That, coupled with his red hair and freckles, gave him a deceptively innocent air. Especially now that I knew he ran freaking sex clubs.

And that he wanted to hold them in *my gallery*.

I'd do anything for Blu. I really would. But a sex party? In my art gallery?

"Yeah, I don't think so. I can't risk it." I took one more bite of my dessert and put my fork down. I had to stop. I scooted my plate toward Blu.

He'd finished his own, already.

"Shit, Av, did it occur to you that this might bring you some new *art* collectors? I'm serious, our vetting process eliminates all but the city's highest rollers. These people buy art. Lots of it, for lots of money."

Um, no, I had not considered that.

How stupid was I?

He continued his sales pitch. "See? This could be beneficial to you in more than one way."

He pushed my tiramisu back toward me, and handed me my fork, as if that would sway my decision.

My resolve was melting, dammit.

"Do you think I could maybe check out one of the parties? Just to see what they're like?" I mean, what was the harm?

He slammed his hand on the table. "Now you're talking, baby. I'll take you to one."

My mind immediately flew to the all-important question of what I would wear. Normally, I'd feel free to go out shopping, but with Devon cutting me off, well it looked like I'd be making do with what was currently hanging in my closet. I actually might not be able to shop for a while, when I stopped and thought about it.

So I pushed the tiramisu back to Blu. I wasn't taking any chances on my clothes not fitting. At least until I knew I could shop again.

I leaned toward him with my hands folded under my chin. "Tell me more."

8

ASH

ANOTHER DRAG-ASS DAY AT THE OFFICE.

The previous night's party had come off without a hitch, and I'd stayed out way too late. The cute blonde waitress from the Hamptons party had come, and boy, was she hot. When she got a load of how sexy the club vibe was, she could hardly keep her hands off us guys. The place did that to some women.

It was like something in them became unleashed—what, I don't really know, but I sure liked being the lucky beneficiary.

I'd just downed another cup of crappy office coffee, and now, my heart was racing. My doctor had told me to stay away from the stuff, but like most people, I'd never get through a day without it.

Sumner and Smith barged into my office.

"Hey, guys, thanks for knocking," I said. Sumner towered over Smith, and with the height disparity between them, they looked like something out of a comic book.

But Smith made up for his challenge in the height area with a big mouth. He burst out laughing. He could be an ass that way.

"Dude, I live in hopes of catching you with some chick bent over your desk, or maybe just your pecker in your hand. That would be awesome." He threw his head back and laughed some more.

"Smith, I didn't know you wanted to see my dick so badly. All you had to do was ask." I stood and made like I was unzipping my pants.

"Kidding, dude! Keep your pants on," he said, the smile fading from his face.

I settled back into my desk chair. "That's what I thought. So what you guys up to, anyway? To what do I owe the pleasure of your barging into my office unannounced?"

"Damn, Ash, quit with the diva bullshit. You walk into our offices all the time," Smith said.

He was a fairly recent addition to the firm, and while there had been some reservations about him, he had a great track record. But he was also annoying as hell.

"Yeah, but I knock first, jerkoff," I said.

Sumner interrupted our bickering. "All right. What are we going to do about Crane Enterprises?"

Huh?

"I hadn't thought there was anything *to* do with them after Gio booted Devon Crane out of our offices," I said.

"Well, it seems he's not quite done with us. He sent over a prospectus and has requested another meeting," Smith explained.

I leaned forward on my desk, speaking slowly and clearly. "Guys, he's under investigation by the D.A."

Sumner threw his hands up. "C'mon, Ash. You know the D.A. is investigating people all the time. It doesn't make him guilty."

"Fair enough. But Gio didn't like the guy. Said he was a scumbag. For Christ's sake, he kicked him out."

"Since when do emotions rule our decisions around here?" he asked, arms crossed.

I sat back in my chair. "I know what you're saying. I really do. But something about this guy feels bad."

"Okay. What do you say to a bit of analysis on the deal? And then we can discuss whether or not we like him," he said with a nod toward Smith. Analysis was Smith's specialty, and I had to hand it to him, he was damn good at it.

"Yeah, whatever. Give it a shot," I said.

My cell rang and when I saw it was Blu, most likely calling about Kink Lab business.

"Hey, Blu," I said.

"Hey, girl," Blu said in his favorite *I will convert you if it's the last thing I do* tone. "Good news. I may have found a solution to our location problem. I didn't get to tell you about it last night because we were so busy."

"Yeah? What's the solution?"

"Well, my best friend, Avril Crane, has a fabulous gallery in Soho that she's considering letting us use for Kink Lab."

Now that was some good news. But shit, Avril Crane? After we were just talking trash about her dickhead ex?

"We were *just* talking about her ex, I kid you not," I said. "But is the space nice?"

Blu cackled. "Why don't you go check it out? I'd like your opinion."

Leaving Smith and Sumner in my office, I headed for the elevator while still on the phone with Blu. We needed a new space fast, and if it was as nice as he said, it would be perfect.

I flagged a cab to head downtown. Yeah, I wanted to see the gallery, but that wasn't the only reason I was going. I'd been curious as hell about the beautiful woman everyone had been talking about at the party.

What might I learn about her, myself?

Naturally, the gallery was on a fashionable street in the Soho neighborhood, long known for its celebrity sightings and galleries showcasing the city's up and coming artists. I walked into the sprawling space Blu had given me the address for, and a bell jingled, announcing my arrival.

A tall woman with long black hair came to greet me.

Damn. She'd looked nice from across the lawn, but in person, she was stunning.

"Hello. May I help you with something today?"

So far, so good. "Hi. I'm Ashera Singh. I wanted to visit the gallery. You and I have actually met before."

She broke into a gorgeous smile that almost brought me to my knees. I knew she must have been going through hell, and yet, she was as poised as anyone I'd ever seen.

"Right. I saw you at that party in the Hamptons." Something sad flashed across her face, but it was gone as quickly as it came. "Would you like to have a look around, then?"

Not pushy. I liked that.

"I would…but I have another reason for being here."

Her eyebrows raised. "You do?"

Might as well get right to the point. "A friend of yours, Blu Baker, is one of my partners in our party promotion company. He suggested I take a look at your gallery to rent for our events." I kept it vague. Who knew if he'd told her exactly what kind of parties we threw?

But it quickly became evident that he had, because her face changed from pink to red in about five seconds. And damn if that didn't get my imagination racing.

"Right! Right, we talked about that. I'm not sure, though—"

"Ms. Crane, did he explain to you that each time we used your location, your cut of the revenues would be somewhere around one hundred thousand dollars?"

Her mouth opened, but nothing came out.

He had not told her *that* part, it seemed.

"Ms. Crane, is there somewhere we could sit and talk?"

The poor woman looked faint.

"Oh yes, I'm sorry. Where are my manners? Please come to my office."

I followed her tight dress and fuck me pumps up some stairs to a loft, where her office was tucked into a corner. She sat at her desk and motioned for me to take the chair opposite.

"Now, what were you saying, um…"

"Ashera. You can call me Ash."

"Oh, right. And you can call me Avril."

"Pretty name," I said.

"It's French for April," she said.

I actually already knew that but didn't say anything. "Cool. So Blu told you about our Kink Lab parties, then?"

She blushed again, and it was damn cute. Picking up a pencil, she began to tap back and forth, like a seesaw.

"Yes, Blu told me about the parties, your security,

and how the cleaning crew moves the furniture in and out. But to be honest, I'm still not sure about having it here. We have some pretty valuable art, and I'm responsible for all of it. But…for a hundred grand per party, I could possibly be convinced to take it down and put it in the safe."

Now she was talking.

"Do you mind if I look around?" I asked. "It just so happens, I'm in the market for some art for my foyer."

I knew that would get her. Plus, my walls really did need some art.

"Please. Make yourself at home. I'll leave you alone for a few minutes while I return some phone calls."

The place was cavernous. I could only imagine what her monthly rent was. And if her soon to be ex was the douche I thought he was, she needed cash, and she needed it fast.

Thick velvet curtains were suspended in front of the floor-to-ceiling loft windows. Perfect for privacy. The hardwood floors were of old, wide planks, worn by decades of footsteps. The effect was industrial and organic. And it was perfect. It would hold all our furniture and props with room to spare. I had to hand it to Blu for fast thinking.

Now, to convince her to join our team. And other things.

"Avril, I've looked around. The place is amazing. I hope you're seriously considering working with us. We could take you on as a partner," I said.

Her eyebrows raised. "A partner? I didn't know that was part of the offer."

"What do you think?" I asked.

"I think…that I'd like to attend a party first, at your current location, to see what they're all about."

Another Blu idea, most likely.

"Excellent. Can I count on seeing you then?" I asked.

"I think so. Yes. Yes, I'll go," she said.

"Now, can you show me some pieces for my apartment?" I asked.

AN HOUR LATER, we were having a glass of wine in Avril's office.

She'd shown me the pieces in her gallery she thought I'd be interested in once I'd clumsily explained my taste in art and what my home looked like. I could learn a lot from that woman.

"Well, Avril," I said, putting down my glass to head out. "I think I'll go with the first piece you showed me. Can I convince you to deliver it in person? I'd like to get your take on the best place to hang it, if you're available for that."

She stood and walked me to the door. "I'd love to help you with that, Ash. I often work with clients to place the pieces they get from us. It's one of the best parts of my job, seeing where our art ends up." She leaned against the wall, hand resting on the doorjamb.

Her earlier nervousness was long gone, replaced by a faint sadness around her eyes that not even her bright smile chased away. I knew how she felt, to be let down by someone she loved.

We all had our stories, didn't we?

I placed my hand over hers on the wall, wrapping my fingers around it. She responded by gripping mine back. Good sign.

"You're very beautiful, Avril."

Her blush returned, with a smile.

She gazed right at me with her dark eyes. "Thank you. I am so glad you stopped by—"

She didn't get to finish because I leaned toward her and kissed her cheek, close enough to her mouth that she stopped talking and made the sweetest little sigh.

I slid my lips toward hers, lingering just at the corner of her mouth to test her openness. When she turned to place her lips directly on mine, I knew my kiss was welcome and commenced to crush her lips until we had trouble breathing.

I stepped back, stunned by the connection. I could have stood there and kissed her all night. But there'd be time for that later.

I had good news for the guys. And not only about the venue for our parties.

9

<hr>

AVRIL

Holy mother of god. I was going to a sex party with a gay guy in just a few hours. If that wasn't the craziest thing.

What was also crazy was, since Devon had given me the heave-ho, how many of our friends had followed his lead.

My two girl-buddies from Pilates class had conveniently taken spots on the other side of the room from where we usually worked out together.

The charity fundraiser I was involved with suddenly had all the volunteers it needed, and my weekly girls' lunch had been mysteriously cancelled, to be rescheduled for a future, unknown date. One they'd conveniently forget to tell me about, I suspected.

Was I surprised? No, not really. Was I hurt? I

supposed so. But like I told Devon, this group of people liked its money more than its friends. Without money, they didn't want me. It was that simple.

They could all rot in hell. I had better things on my mind.

I didn't exactly know what to expect of the sex party, but I knew I wanted to look my best. Apparently not even a broken heart trumped my vanity.

I still stung badly thanks to Devon's betrayal, but the kiss I'd gotten from Blu's handsome partner Ash, even though it was kind of a quickie, had just about bowled me over. I didn't think Devon had *ever* kissed me like that, so softly, all exploration, while also giving me the chance to red or green light it.

And Ash's dark and exotic looks only added to the thrill.

I didn't know him well, but I did know he was part of a very successful partnership of guys who'd been together at college. They were a popular group of single men and handsome enough to look like they walked out of an Abercrombie ad or something. It was just amazing.

I'm sure they were big hits with the ladies. Being a married woman myself, I didn't really pay attention to that stuff.

Although, it looked like I was maybe going to start.

The painting Ash had bought had been my absolute favorite in the gallery. I would be lying if I didn't admit to being a bit envious. I would also be lying if I didn't say I was looking forward to helping him hang it in his apartment.

Before I left home, the one I supposed I might be evicted from, I smoothed down the front of my red Diane von Furstenberg wrap dress, making sure my thong left no visible lines under it. I adjusted my strappy skyscraper heels. I would be towering over Blu, which always seemed funny to me. Not so much to him.

At nine o'clock sharp, just as Blu had instructed, the limo dropped me at the party.

I climbed several steps to a plain blue door and rang the bell. I was greeted by a woman in a bustier, stockings, and high heels. Her makeup looked like something out of a Cirque du Soleil show, always a favorite of mine.

I wondered if I could try a look like that.

"Baby!" Blu screamed, running toward me with his arms out. Standing on his toes, he gave me a big hug, which was exactly what I needed at that moment.

He looked me up and down. "You look fucking hot, girl. You could have any guy here you wanted. But we know that's not what you are here for." He winked and gave me his best smirk.

Smart ass.

He was right, though. Men were *not* what I was there for. It was all about due diligence. Making smart business decisions. Nothing more.

He took my hand, and we passed through several

gossamer curtains hanging from the ceiling, fluttering in the room's slight breeze. We entered a foyer of sorts, and when we turned the corner, I found what I'd been waiting for.

I had to be honest. I'd Googled sex clubs. I had to learn what I could before I set foot in one. Turned out they were all over the damn place.

Newsflash.

Had I been out of the loop, or what?

I'd had a boyfriend after college try to tell me he'd once been to one with a wealthy, older lady. He said they'd gotten there and been required to remove their clothes. They wore towels the rest of the night.

As you can imagine, I told him he was full of shit. Why didn't he just try to sell me the Brooklyn Bridge while he was at it?

Now I felt kind of bad about doubting him. Not that bad, though. He'd turned out to be a cheater, just like my husband.

And now, I was at a sex club. A freaking sex club. With my gay best friend, who—by the way—hosted the parties with a group of *straight* men who were part of my social circle. Or what was left of it.

How bizarre was that? And what if I ran into someone I knew?

Whatever. I had nothing to hide. I was there for business.

But when we turned the corner, what I saw before me made me wobble in my high heels.

In the center of the small room we entered—the lofty space seemed to be broken into cozy little rooms —was a big, round sofa.

In the middle of it was a man going to town on a woman whose dress was pushed up to her waist. As he licked and sucked her, he ran his hands over her hips and ass in a smooth motion that increased her writhing pleasure.

I'd only watched a porno once before, before Devon had gotten up and turned it off in disgust. To be honest, I'd wanted to see more but was too embarrassed to speak up at the time.

So here I was now, watching two other people go at it, live and in person. And when I glanced around the room, I realized they weren't the only ones having some fun.

I felt a nudge against my elbow.

"Well? What do you think?" Blu asked, his face as excited as a little boy on Christmas morning.

My face must have said it all, because he grabbed my hand and led me to chair that I just about collapsed into.

"Wait right here. I'll run to get us some bubbly," he said.

Holy lord. I don't know what I'd expected, but this was really something.

I loved it.

Oh god. Was that bad?

Tough shit. I was making changes in my life,

starting now.

Blu came back with two flutes of champagne. I pressed mine against my forehead for a sec, and then enjoyed a nice, big swig.

It was the good stuff. 'Course for what people paid to get into Kink Lab, they had to offer top-shelf beverages.

What had Blu told me people paid for each party? Wasn't it something like two thousand dollars each? If I hosted at my gallery, half of that money would be mine.

I had a feeling he'd negotiated an especially good deal for me due to my situation. And he also knew that made it harder for me to say *no*.

LUCKY FOR ME, I'd gotten in for free. I certainly was not in a position to throw around two *hundred* dollars, much less two thousand dollars.

So fuck that jerk Devon for cutting me off, and yeah, I was getting more comfortable with the F-bomb.

It was a great relief knowing I didn't have to worry about running into him at Kink Lab. He could barely make love with the lights on, never mind in public, whether participating or just watching. The scene there would have made his head explode, no doubt.

"So....?" Blu asked, clearly hoping for good news.

I took a deep breath to steady my nerves. The champagne was helping. "Whew. It's really something. I mean, I'm not even sure what to say."

Somehow, I'd already downed my first glass. "Do you think I could have another?" I asked Blu, handing him my empty flute.

He was up and back in a flash. I guess when you're one of the owner-promoters, you don't have to wait in line at the bar.

"Dontcha think it's hot?" he asked, sidling up to me.

I looked at him. "The question is, why would *you* think it's hot? I don't see a gay man for miles."

"Ah. Yes. I get what you're saying. You see, Av, it's sexy not because I have any interest whatsoever in watching Barbie and Ken over there get it on." He pointed toward a couple who did, really, look like a human Barbie and Ken. "What I'm getting at is that the sex-positive vibe, even if it's not my team that's play-ing"—he looked around, turning his nose up a little— "is still erotic as hell. Ya know?"

No, I didn't know.

"Okay. Let me put it more plainly. I'm not inter-ested in watching Ken's schlong pump in and out of Barbie's shaved beaver over there." He craned his neck and shook his head as if he couldn't imagine how any man would want to do that with a woman.

Then he turned back to me. "But it's really hot to witness their pleasure. I mean, look at their faces."

"Okay, okay, I get it. Then why don't you do this for the gay community?"

Seriously.

"Because, my dear," he said as he took my hand and patted it like I was a senile old lady. "For every *one* club like this, there are probably *a hundred* gay ones. Because of that, there's not the same kind of money in it. We've already been over this."

"I guess. I mean, I can see how profitable this is when people pay two thousand a head to get in," I said.

"Exactly. You can go to a gay sex club party for next to nothing. Us fags like to hump early and often, and there are many opportunities to do that."

Good old supply and demand. I'd never been very good at economics, but this seemed like a perfect case study for making some money. A lot of money.

10

SUMNER

I walked the floor through a party already in full swing.

The guys and I always held Kink Lab on weeknights. Because of that, our guests tended to get there early, take care of business, and leave at a decent hour. Usually, by midnight everyone was gone, and we'd have locked the doors and headed home ourselves.

Which was fine with me because, like everyone else, I had to get up and go to work the next morning.

It took only one of us to close up after the party and supervise the clean up crew, so we took turns.

Whoever stayed late usually came into work the next day around ten a.m. It was hardly sleeping in, but it was something. That particular night, Gio had the late shift. The only one who never did was Chase since he had a baby at home. We were all cool with that.

Smith was not part of this venture. It just didn't seem like the kind of energy he'd bring would be...I guess you could say *conducive* to a sexy atmosphere.

I made my rounds like the rest of the guys, greeting our guests, making the men feel important and the women feel gorgeous. For what they were paying to attend, it was the least we could do.

There were some *seriously* important and beautiful people there. From where I stood, I watched several prominent New Yorkers mixing and mingling as a sort of warm up to the main event.

Speaking of watching, I'd spotted Blu come in with his friend and potential future party host, Avril. Good grief, she was a looker. They were sitting across the room on a couple of the cushy chairs we brought in for the parties. While Blu talked her ear off, she looked around the room in awe. I knew what that was like.

The first time I went to a sex party, I was astounded, too.

Turned on as hell, and completely blown away. The eroticism was not like anything I'd ever seen in any porno. Nothing about it was staged. The sensuality flowed through the room as people sucked and fucked, and I tried not to stare like some kind of amateurish asshole.

That was one of the ways to spot a newbie. They stared.

Sex party etiquette dictated you could look around, of course, but you had to be discreet about it so as not to make anyone feel uncomfortable. Most people at sex parties, when they were butt naked and getting it on, enjoyed being watched—why else would they be there? —but they didn't want to be creeped out by someone with no game.

But that was okay, because most people caught on pretty quick, and those who didn't weren't invited back. Pretty simple.

So even though the beautiful Avril was still fully clothed, and would probably remain so the entire night since she was only scoping out our business proposition, I didn't let her catch me staring. In fact, when she finally did meet my eye, I waved and moved on to another room.

I'd made the mistake—at least, I think it was a mistake—of inviting the cute blonde server from the Hamptons party, as our guest.

She came with an equally cute friend, and they were throwing themselves at a well-known city council member. He appeared to be enjoying himself, but they were really pounding the booze, and I wasn't sure things were going to end well.

Sometimes I felt like a damn babysitter, but I was well paid for the effort. All of us guys were. We just needed a new venue.

Time to chat up the lovely Avril.

On my way over to her, I ran into Gio and Chase.

"Hey, that's Avril over there with Blu, right?" Chase asked.

Ash joined us. "Oh yeah, that's Avril. Amazing, isn't she? I went to see her at her gallery."

All heads whipped in Ash's direction.

"Yeah?"

"Nice space?"

"Good art?"

He smiled quietly as he always did. "The place was awesome, in fact perfect, and exactly what we are looking for," Ash said. "I bought a nice painting and got a sweet kiss on my way out."

"Ah. She is a *bella signorina,* for sure," Gio said.

"Sum, what the fuck is wrong with her husband? He needs to have his head examined," Chase said, frowning.

I shook my head. "No idea. He's crazy to let someone like that get away. Speaking of which, Chase, Gio, let's go meet a potential business partner. We're gonna go chat her up and see what she's thinking of our little proposition."

"That's not our only proposition," Ash called after us.

"Sum!" Blu called when he saw me approaching.

Blu helped Avril to her feet, and she held on to him tightly.

What was that all about?

But I didn't have to wonder for long.

She teetered in her high heels. "Hi, I'm Avril!" she

exclaimed, grasping my hand in both of hers, then introducing herself to Chase and Gio.

"Hey there girlie, don't knock my brothers over." Blu gave her a stern look and straightened her up.

She shook her head, which seemed to slightly clear the cobwebs. "Sorry. I guess I'm a teeny bit buzzed."

I ran my hand across her shoulder and reached for the long hair behind her back.

She watched me pull a handful of it to her front, where I strategically let it drop, fanning over her left breast. When I let go, her gaze floated from my hand up to my eyes, where we stared at each other for several seconds. I hadn't seen dark eyes that beautiful since—well—ever.

Blu watched the whole thing, unsure of what to do. He was usually happy for us guys to pursue a beautiful woman, but he was clearly protective of this one. I could respect that. I sort of felt the same way, and I barely knew her.

"What do you think of our club, Avril? Do you like it so far?" Chase asked.

She looked down for a second, then back up at us. "I do. It's kind of shocking at first, but then you get used to it. It's beautiful to see people enjoying themselves like this."

Yes. She got it.

"Right?" Blu asked. "I mean, I could give a shit about straight sex. In fact, it's kind of gross, if you ask me.

But there's something so sexy in the air at these parties."

"Not to mention the money to be made, right Blu?" I added quietly.

He nodded.

"C'mon, let me show you around." I extended my arm for her to hold. "Guys, do you mind excusing us for a bit?" I asked.

"Not at all Sum, you crazy kids go have fun. I have some meeting and greeting of my own to do." He blew us both a kiss and scooted off, followed by Chase and Ash, totally comfortable leaving Avril in my qualified hands.

"We'll catch up later, Sum," Gio said, amused, watching Blu skip off into the crowd.

Avril and I walked to the second floor of the venue where Kink Lab was being held for the last time.

"It's a shame you can't use this place again," Avril said. "It's just perfect."

"It is. It really is. But the building's being turned into condos." I turned to her, holding her arms. "But Ash told me he visited your gallery, and that it was the perfect alternative."

Even in the dark, I could see her turn several shades of pink.

"Oh. Ash told you he came by?" she said, like she'd been caught doing something nasty.

I had to nip any concerns like that in the bud, and

quickly. "He also told us he bought an amazing painting. And that he kissed you."

She pulled out of my grasp and started to walk away.

"Avril, please. Wait."

She whirled around. "Yes, Sumner, I kissed him."

"There's nothing to be embarrassed about."

"I just don't appreciate him telling you that. I'm going through a lot right now, and I don't like being gossiped about."

"He likes you, Avril. So do I."

"Huh?" she asked.

I led her to a sofa in a quiet corner.

"Ash would like to date you. And I would too."

"What?" Confusion muddled her pretty face. "What the hell are you talking about?"

A couple partygoers floated by, completely naked, nodding as if the were just passing us on the street.

"The four of us, actually—I'm including Chase and Gio—we share. We like to date the same woman."

She wrinkled her nose. "Share? One woman? What? I don't get it."

"It started when we were in college. Gio and I always like the same girls, so we would date one if we found she that was into it. It worked out great. And over the years, Chase and Ash realized they liked the same women we did."

She shook her head. "I don't think I understand."

"I get that. There's a lot going on. I mean, here we

are at a sex party." I gestured toward a woman on her knees, servicing a very happy man.

She looked around the party. I'd thrown her off, and I felt a little bad about that. But anyone would be thrown off by a night like the one we were having.

"No pressure, Avril, about hosting Kink Lab, or anything else. But I do hope you'll consider the gallery as a place to host."

She looked down at her hands, so I hooked my finger under her chin to meet her gaze.

"It's your party, beautiful. You decide whom to invite."

11

AVRIL

It's my party, Sumner had told me.

He was right.

My fucker of a husband had dumped me for my whoring assistant. All our friends acted like I had the plague. My credit cards had been cut off, and I was going to be out of money pretty soon.

The only reason the limo driver was still coming around was that he felt sorry for me. And I knew that was going to end soon.

No time like the present to change things up.

"Yes," I blurted, before I could change my mind.

Sumner tilted his head just the smallest amount, his dimples flashing, then disappearing again into the gorgeous planes of his face.

"Yes, what?" he asked.

"Yes, you can use the gallery. I mean, let's try it once, and see how it goes."

He nodded slowly. "Okay. We'll give it a shot. See what happens."

I looked around the room at the beautiful people milling about. Some were dressed, some were naked. Some were having sex, and some were politely watching.

The woman who'd answered the door earlier in the evening, wearing with the circus-type makeup, flitted by us. She was holding the hand of a man *and* woman and looked like she was on her way to someplace very important.

Well.

Hosting Kink Lab at my gallery might just work.

The guests didn't seem the types to get out of control, so I wouldn't have to worry about my artwork. Of course, it didn't hurt that there were several burly bouncers walking around, discouraging any sort of bad behavior into oblivion.

"I can see you're tired," Sumner said.

Busted.

I'd tried to stifle a yawn, but apparently wasn't as sneaky as I'd thought.

"I'm sorry, Sumner. That was so rude of me. I haven't been sleeping well. I have a lot going on, and I probably had too much champagne." I reached back to rub my neck, stiff from multiple nights of tossing and turning.

He nodded while his sultry gaze studied me. It was unsettling. In a good way.

"Yeah. I guess everyone knows my business these days," I sighed.

"People know *some* of your business. But not *all* of your business." He stood and extended his hand.

I let him pull me to my feet. I was amazed at how my fatigue had suddenly weighted my arms and legs. Funny how that sort of thing sneaks up on you.

"Let me take you home," he offered.

"Okay."

I wasn't sure what he had in mind, but I figured I'd find out pretty quickly.

I'd sent my driver home long ago, so it was nice to have someone hail a cab for me. He followed me into the backseat.

"Oh, I forgot to say goodbye to Blu," I said, reaching for my phone to send a text.

Sumner glanced at his watch. "He usually heads out about this time. He has his own social circle to catch up to."

I gave a small laugh. "Isn't that the truth."

He turned to face me. "Avril, you are so beautiful tonight," He brought my hand up to his mouth and ran his lips across my palm.

Good lord. And the way he looked at me. If I wasn't careful, I might melt right there on the backseat of the cab.

He smoothed his fingers across my cheek to reach

my hair, letting them tangle in and out of it. Devon had done that when we were first married, but I could no longer remember the last time he had.

Sumner's hand, expansive and strong, was warm, actually *hot* against the back of my neck. I let my eyes flutter closed and dropped my head against him.

When I turned my face to look at him, he brushed a light kiss over my lips. And almost before I could register what he'd done, he was already looking out the cab window again, the streetlights flashing over his face as we passed each one.

That was all I was going to get?

I screwed up all my courage. "Would you like to come in with me?" I tried to sound bold and worldly, but I think it might have come out as more of a squeak.

Holy shit, had I really just said that? I immediately regretted it.

But the evening had been so sexy, and Sumner was so damn gorgeous.

And it had been so long…

He ran his hand through his black hair and sighed before looking back at me.

"Yes. I would like to. Actually, I'd love to. But I'm not going to."

Geez. Way to make a girl feel good.

"I will, however, come in with you another night, after I've taken you for a proper evening out, when you are not on the brink of falling asleep, and when you are not already buzzed by several glasses of champagne. I make it a practice to never go home with women under the influence." He smiled down at me.

Goddamn. Where had this man come from?

And he was right. It wasn't the right time. It melted my heart that he respected me enough to want it to be a special evening. We pulled up in front of my building, and he walked me to the door.

"I'd like to have dinner with you this weekend," he said, waiting for me to turn my key in the lock. "And I want to give you a heads up that Chase may be calling you, too. Actually, all the guys probably will."

I still didn't get it.

But I was too tired to belabor the point. I'd try to figure it all out later, when I wasn't so pooped.

I had plenty of time on my hands now that I was *persona non grata* in my old community, so what was the harm in hanging out with gorgeous men who were all friends, all wanted to date me, and who all knew about each other?

Okay, that was just crazy talk. But at least I couldn't get in trouble for being deceitful. Unlike some people…

And the way Sumner had kissed, his lips soft but confident. Like a man who knew who he was, and what he could get done…

After our good-nights, I walked as quickly as I could through the lobby to the elevator. I was afraid if I didn't move fast enough, I wouldn't make it to bed. As it was, once inside my apartment—the one I used to share with a husband—I threw my clothes on the floor, climbed under the sheets completely naked, and pulled my fluffy down comforter up to my ears. My mind turned off almost immediately.

Unfortunately, my dreams did not.

Since she'd left me, Lisette liked to visit my dreams.

Whether she was really there or my imagination had just conjured her because I missed her so terribly, I'd never been entirely sure. But the dreams alternated between comforting and disturbing. I never knew what I was going to get and consequently, they were a constant source of worry.

In my dream that particular night, which was the same as in so many others, we were driving, laughing, talking, and I was trying to fix her hair—just as we had been on that fateful day. The problem was, I was also driving the car.

As we did our usual sister thing, I flew through a traffic light. All I know about what followed was that we collided with something big, heavy, and loud.

Lisette didn't make it. I almost didn't, but I managed to survive with several broken bones and a closed head injury.

But in my dream, Lisette *did* live. And instead of her dying and my being severely injured, when we crashed, the car spun several times. It bounced off other things in the road, exactly what, I wasn't sure, and when we came to a stop, she looked at me.

"Holy shit. That could have been bad."

I was so scared, I was shivering, and we held hands

until our knuckles turned white. But we were okay, and we were together.

If only.

I WOKE with the morning sun elbowing its way into my room as if it were my own personal, torturous alarm clock.

Thank goodness my dreams were behind me—well, they were never really *that* far behind me—and I could dive into the distracted busyness that daylight brought. I threw on my clothes and called my car for a ride down to the gallery.

Funny thing was, the driver didn't answer.

So I called again.

Guess he was gone. Fucking Devon. Didn't even have the balls to tell me ahead of time. How was it I married someone who turned out to be such a piece of human garbage? It was so puzzling, not to mention downright painful.

I'd had a husband whom I thought loved me. He'd been nice, kind, and supportive. What makes a person change on a dime?

But I pushed those thoughts out of my head. I needed a break from the shitty days I'd been having, and I was going to make this a good one if it goddamn killed me. As soon as I was dressed, I ran out in front of my building and caught a cab.

Twenty minutes later, as I was unlocking the heavy door to my gallery, I heard the phone ringing from the other side. I got to it just in time.

"Took you long enough," Blu said, his voice full of sleep.

"Blu! Good morning, sweetie," I said, really laying it on. I knew that would irritate him to no end. "How late were you out last night?"

"You don't want to know, Av. But I can tell you, it was worth it."

"Well then, I'm happy for you." I locked the gallery door behind me. I had two hours before opening, and I had a ton of office work to catch up on now that my whoring ex-assistant wasn't around to help.

He yawned in my ear. "Enough with the pleasantries. Tell me what you thought of the club."

I chose my words carefully. It was his business and his livelihood, after all.

"I gotta tell you," I said, "it was…it was incredible. I mean, it was weird at first, but when I got used to watching people—you know—"

"Av, say it. F-U-C-K-I-N-G. People were *fucking.* You're thirty years old. You gotta start using the F-bomb like you own it," he said.

"Okay. Okay, then. I liked watching the fucking. It was hot as hell."

"There's my girl. I knew you weren't born yesterday, even if you'd spent the last three years of your life married to the biggest tight-ass in Manhattan."

"Okay then. Fuck fuck fuckity fuck. Are you happy now?"

He cackled so loudly that I had to pull the phone from my ear.

"I knew there was hope for you, Av. I will teach you to be a dirty girl, just like me. You'll be whoring around before you know it."

"Um, well, I don't really think so—"

"Anyway," he interrupted, "what about the guys?"

Ugh. I knew he was going to go there.

"What do you mean?" I asked to stall for time.

"You know what I mean," he said slowly.

Yeah. I guess I did.

"Sumner told me a bit about their particular… tendencies," I said.

"Mmm hmm. I bet he did. So what are you gonna do?" he asked.

"Blu, if you knew these guys were into this stuff, why didn't you ever say anything to me? You know, give me a heads up?"

"Oh. I see. It's my job to give you a heads up that a harem of men might be interested in you? Well, I tell you what, missy…"

I braced myself for a scolding.

"…I can't out those guys for their particular proclivities just like you can't out me for being gay. And, are you kidding? Of course, they were gonna like you. You're amazing."

"Well, thank you. Anyway, no one needs to out you for being gay." I said.

He hmphed. "I'll take that as a compliment, thankyouverymuch. But back to you. You're a big girl. You don't need me to warn you about boys."

"Well, it might have been nice to know they're into this *sharing* thing."

"Look, Av. They are a nice, good-looking bunch, and I've known them for many years. I wish they played for my team, but I gave up on that long ago. If you like them, date them. If not, move on."

Move on? He was right, I guessed.

But I wasn't sure I wanted to.

12

CHASE

Our Kink Lab party from the night before had been a smashing success, as always.

I hadn't stayed until the end because I wanted to get home to my baby girl, but we'd had about a hundred and fifty guests—our largest party to date—and everything came off smooth as silk.

'Course, it was no accident when things worked out well. We busted our asses to ensure everything fell perfectly into place for our guests. After all, if you were paying two thousand dollars to attend a party, you'd expect it to be fucking perfect, too.

And the best news was that the lovely Avril was willing to let us test-drive an event at her gallery. According to Ash and Blu, it was the perfect space for

Kink Lab, even better than the loft where we'd been holding it for the last two years.

Every cloud has a silver lining, I supposed...

I'd never worried about finding a new venue for the parties. New York was chock-full of fascinating old buildings. I knew it would just take some work to find the perfect one. And then Avril's gallery just fell into our lap, thanks to good old Blu.

But the absolute best thing Blu did was bring Avril into our lives.

Yeah, it was early days, but I had a good feeling about her.

I mean, sure, we were part of the same general social circle and all. I recognized her because I'd seen her around—usually with her cocksucker husband— but I didn't *know* her at all.

The minute Blu started talking about her, I saw her in a different light. One where she wasn't in the shadow of an unappreciative husband, or just some other spoiled, rich wife, but where she was a smart, accomplished woman with her own business, whose life had just been unexpectedly shit on by some of the people closest to her.

She'd earned her battle scars, just like we guys had. And I liked that.

Sumner had let me know he'd dropped our 'bomb' on Avril. I say that because you never know how someone will react to the idea of being *shared*. So far, so good—she hadn't run away screaming. 'Course she hadn't signed on the dotted line, either.

I'd watched her from across the room at the party the previous night, letting Blu ease her into the sex club vibe. Everyone reacted differently their first time.

Some people went apeshit wild, tearing off their clothes and wanting to fuck everything in sight. Some people stood in a dark corner, wondering what the hell they were doing there. Most people fell somewhere in between. They were, without a doubt, intrigued and maybe dying to jump in, but they also took their time easing into whatever it was that turned them on.

Avril was one of those people in the middle. They were the best kind, in my opinion. Gutsy but wise enough to get the lay of the land first.

So it had probably come as no surprise to her when I called her the morning after the party to ask her to lunch. I did it on the pretense of discussing business, but if I could steer things in a more intimate direction, so much the better. The guys had asked me to seal the deal, at least with regard to securing the gallery for our next party.

But if I could interest her in our amorous intentions, everyone would be happy. Especially her, I liked to think.

When I arrived at the gallery, I entered through a huge, heavy door. The building had most likely once been something industrial. The owners had clearly tried to keep some of the place's old charms intact.

It was huge and sunny, with twenty-foot high ceilings and wide wooden boards for hardwood floors. Low voices floated through the air, and while I couldn't make out what they were saying, I could detect Avril's voice and that of the clients she'd told me she'd be meeting with that morning.

I grabbed a seat on the cushy sofa in the corner and opened the phone app that allowed me to check in on Ruby when she was napping in her crib. *Voila,* there was my gorgeous little girl. She was lying in that funny position babies do, where they're flat on their backs with their arms reaching overhead. Her face was turned to the side, and I had to say, her profile was so goddamn beautiful, I got a lump in my throat.

Funny how one of the worst things to ever happen to you can turn out to be one of the best. Little Ruby's mom might have bailed on us, but our baby had brought more joy into my life than I ever knew was possible.

I watched Avril escort two men, the couple she'd been discussing the artwork with, to the door. She shook their hands.

When she turned to me, her face brightened.

"Hello!" she said, clicking across the room toward me in her stiletto heels.

She wore a plain, black knit dress that clung to her every curve. On anyone else, it might have looked like a sack, but on her curvy figure, it was perfection.

The woman was gorgeous by any measure, but to

see her in her element, conducting business like a champ, only added to the appeal that left me wanting so badly. The rest of the guys often teased me that a shift in the wind got me hard, but this was the real thing.

I stood to kiss her cheek, lingering for a moment to experience her light perfume. Christ, it was going to be hard to keep the conversation to business.

"The gallery is amazing," I said, looking around.

She nodded. "Thank you. It's my baby. I love it too."

I could have sworn I saw something wistful wash over her pretty face. "Are you okay?" I asked.

She pursed her lips before answering. "Well, I've had some concerns about whether or not I'll be able to keep it going. I mean, that's why Blu brought us all together."

That wasn't the only reason. He knew our tastes as well as we did.

"That's one of the things we'll talk about over lunch then," I said, smiling. "Shall we go?"

Just a few minutes later, we settled into a window table at the best steakhouse in the city. It also happened to be owned by a frequent guest at Kink Lab. He'd stopped by the table to thank me for a great time the night before.

What could I say? We aimed to please.

"I guess I should have asked first if you ate meat."

She reached across the table and patted my arm. "It's all good. I love it, actually."

"Whew. Thank goodness. I wouldn't want you to think I was an asshole. At least, not yet. Wine?" I asked.

"Yes, I could totally go for a glass of wine."

We ordered, and the waiter scurried away.

"Thank you for joining me for lunch," I said.

She blushed the tiniest bit. Goddamn, that was cute.

"I've always wanted to try this place."

"So tell me about the gallery," I said.

She nodded as the waiter opened our bottle and poured. "I used to be an art teacher. Before I got married."

Her happy face faltered for a moment, but she rallied. With a deep inhale, she pulled her shoulders back and plunged into her story.

"After I married, I began volunteering at the children's art center. I met several gallery owners and worked for one part-time for a year. That owner retired, and my husband suggested we buy the business."

She took a bite of her pork chop. "Oh, my god. This is heaven. Anyway, it's been a kind of hobby job until now. It's yet to be profitable. We do okay, but with the cost of rent and other expenses here in Manhattan, my husband always supplemented things. He never minded. But that's changed now."

She shook her head.

"Shit. That's a lot of pressure."

And she was right. Our lunch *was* incredible. I'd have to compliment the owner next time I saw him at one of our parties. It was funny to see someone working a dining room whom you'd watched doing sixty-nine with a woman just the night before.

She continued, "So, things might be looking up for the gallery if hosting your parties works out…"

"Avril, this could be very lucrative for you."

"It sounds like it. I'm giving it a shot. We'll see how it all goes."

"That's great news. We'll iron out all the details in the next few days, but you won't be sorry. In fact, this could be good for you in many ways."

"Like I might get more clients for the gallery," she said with a hopeful smile.

"I think there's a strong chance of that."

We ate in silence for a few more minutes, and I refilled both our wine glasses.

"So, I understand you have a baby," she said. "Blu told me."

"I do. The light of my life." Sounded sappy, but I couldn't help it. Nor did I care. "Her name's Ruby."

"I'll bet she's gorgeous."

"I think so."

"Where's her mom?"

"Dunno. She took off. Left me with our little angel. And good riddance to her," I said, raising my glass.

Avril toasted me back. "Ruby is lucky to have you."

"Ah. I'm lucky to have her."

I grabbed the check and found our wine had been comped. One of the fringe benefits of my life…

"Shall we head out?" I asked.

We walked back to the gallery, and when we were inside, I locked the door behind us.

"Do you have any more appointments today, Avril?" I asked, leaning my back against the heavy door.

She gave me a shy smile. "No. I was just going to do some paperwork this afternoon."

Yes.

I walked toward her, slowly and deliberately. "You know, when I saw you at that Hamptons party, I really wanted to talk to you."

"Why didn't you?" she asked, tilting her head.

"You looked so alone. It didn't seem like the right time to chat you up. Plus, you were married."

"Good thinking. That was quite the day," she said.

I leaned toward her, and our lips met for the first time. As soon as they did, I knew it would not be for the last time.

In fact, I knew there would be many, many more times.

But because she didn't know that yet, I would be patient.

13

AVRIL

Wow. Chase Roman. Blond, dark-eyed, clean-shaven with a delicious little cleft in his baby-faced chin.

And a single dad.

That was some seriously grown-up stuff. A man, raising a daughter on his own. To be honest, it made my problems pale in comparison.

And when our lips met, well, I knew I had to know more about this man. He was part of a great group of guys.

Three of whom I'd now kissed—Ash, Sumner, and now Chase. Would Gio be next?

God, I was feeling slutty, but what was the harm in kissing? And they all knew about it, so there would be no deceiving going on.

"C'mon," I said, taking Chase's hand, emboldened by the hand life had dealt me.

If anyone had told me just a few weeks ago I'd be lusting after a man—actually, men—other than my husband, well, I never would have believed them. Not in a million years.

But I also never would have believed my sister would leave me so young, or that my once-adoring and attentive husband would dump my ass.

I led Chase to my office in the loft. I'd filled it with lots of white, slipcovered furniture. Not very practical, I knew, but I'd wanted something girly to soften the industrial feel of it.

"It's nice up here," Chase said, looking around.

"Thanks," I said.

The new Avril was taking no prisoners. No, I had things to accomplish, and that included spending time with this gorgeous man.

And possibly his friends. In a sex club. That also happened to be my gallery.

Chase's lips hit mine, and the stress in my body dribbled away. I didn't know where it went, or if it would come back, but for that moment in time, I felt better than I had in ages. Better than I had when I was married. Almost better than I had before my sister died.

He pulled me to him, gently enough to let me know I could turn him away at any time, if I wanted to.

Which I didn't.

I opened my lips to accept more of him, and wouldn't you know, that hot and bothered feeling between my legs started up, just like it had when I'd kissed the other guys.

Boy, I was in for some trouble.

He ran kisses down the side of my neck, while grasping handfuls of my ass and squeezing.

Just as I was contemplating tearing my dress off, he excused himself, explaining he had to get back to work.

What was it with these guys?

CHASE HADN'T WASTED any time in setting a date for the next Kink Lab. I'd be lying if said I wasn't a nervous wreck. I mean, I couldn't afford to have the one thing in my life right now that was worth anything, damaged or destroyed. They'd all promised there'd be no problems, but I was leaving nothing to chance.

The party's 'advance men,' as they called them, arrived at four in the afternoon, several hours before the actual event was to start.

I'd already stored the gallery's most expensive artwork in a locked closet, just in case. I watched the movers take over my gallery with an efficient expertise, emptying their moving truck of furniture into the place in less than thirty minutes.

Then, Blu appeared on the scene to tell the movers

what to place where. Using my ladder, they even hung some filmy fabric from the pipes running across the ceiling.

The transformation was incredible. My gallery was now ready for a sex club.

"Whew, that was a lot of work. But the place looks fucking great," Blu said, plopping down into one of the several fluffy sofas he'd brought in.

"It really does," I said, looking around in disbelief.

"Hey, Av, you look nervous. Relax, why dontcha? When the party ends at midnight, the crew returns, moves everything back into the truck, and cleans the place from top to bottom. When you come in tomorrow morning, you'll never know anything happened here," he said.

I took a deep breath. "I hope so, Blu. I really do."

He grabbed my hand and pulled me down on the sofa next to him. "Av, sweetie. Trust me on this. Have I ever let you down?"

"Well, you let me marry Devon even though you thought he was a jerk."

He nodded. "Okay. I did let you down in that area. But I'm not going to any more. Promise." He held up his small finger for the pinky promise we used when we were looking out for each other.

I loved him for that. And the funny thing was, it really did make me feel better.

"So, on to more important topics. What are you

wearing tonight?" he asked, waving his hand over me like a fairy godmother.

Which, he sort of was.

"Well, um, I was just gonna wear what I have on," I said, checking out my dress and shoes as if I hadn't already done that a dozen times before I'd left the house that morning.

"WHAT?"

"What do you mean *what*? What's wrong with my outfit?"

"*How* many *times* do we have to *go* through this?" he said, drawing out his words like I was some sort of thick-headed toddler. He did that sometimes.

"I think my black sheath dress is perfectly appropriate."

"Okay. It's a *sex* party, not a board meeting of one of your charities. That DVF wrap dress you had on last time was way better."

"I could go home and get that."

"Av, what you don't understand is that this is your place. You are partnering with us guys. You are a *hostess*."

Well. I hadn't thought of it that way. I'd imagined myself perhaps watching from the sidelines, not meeting and greeting.

"Um, okay," I said.

"Here," he said, furiously texting a message on his phone.

"There isn't time, Blu. I'll dress differently for next time."

"There's plenty of time," he shrieked. "Okay. I just texted my boy Juan up at Barneys New York. Is your driver nearby?"

I wished. "No. Asshole cut me off from him, too."

"What a fucker. Okay, then. We'll go out front, and I'll hail you a cab. Meet Juan in the designer department at Barneys. He'll have a dressing room full of clothes for you to try."

"All right, boss. Whatever you say."

"He'll also extend to you the fuck-buddy discount he gives me. Just this once, though," he added, shaking a finger at me.

I really didn't need to know about Blu's fuck-buddy discounts.

Although, I wondered if he got one at Bendel's, too.

NOT TWO HOURS LATER, I was back at the gallery, where Blu was giving last minute instructions to the beautiful young women who'd be tending the bars.

They were all wearing cute little getups of suit jackets and bow ties with nothing underneath. Not even trousers. Thigh-high stockings and stilettos finished the look with mini top hat fascinators.

Could I pull off a look like that?

Blue came rushing up to me and tore the shopping bags from my hands. "Lemme see! Lemme see!" he said, greedily.

Tissue paper and fabric began to fly as he approved my—or should I say Juan's?—selections.

I lowered my voice. "I like what the bartenders are wearing. Maybe I could try a getup like that?"

"NO! Not only NO but HELL NO." He looked around and then lowered his own voice. "You are *not* one of the hired help. Do you understand that?" he hissed.

Geez. Maybe I was a novice in this business, but he didn't have to talk to me like I was an abject idiot.

He rustled through the three different outfits I'd chosen and settled on one.

"Oh, my freaking god," he shrieked. "I *knew* Juan would hook you up," he said, waving a red crushed velvet dress around like it was a victory flag.

"Give me that. You'll mess it up," I said, grabbing it from him.

"Av, tomorrow when you wake up, you will be a hundred grand richer, and that's only the beginning. Now go put on that goddam thing before I divorce you as my best friend."

I WAS NO SOONER in my new dress and sky-high heels when the guests started to arrive. I was already a bit nervous, but when people began pouring in the door, I thought I might lose it.

I spotted Blu from across the room. "Oh my god, we can't have this many people here," I whispered. "What are we going to do?"

He took a step back, his gaze running me up and down.

"Now that is more like it. You are fucking *hot*."

I had to admit, I felt pretty good.

"Thank you," I said, proudly. "Now what about all these people?" I whispered.

"Oh, you're fine," he said, dismissing me with a hand. "We have no more than our usual hundred-fifty or so. I think folks are coming early because they're excited about the new place. We really played it up in the email invite."

Well, damn. That's why people were so eager to get here. I guessed a new venue was kind of like new meat.

Except that this was *my* meat.

14

GIO

CHE DONNA!

When Avril greeted me at the door, my Italian sensibilities were dumbstruck. I'd always appreciated a *bellissima* woman—as Italian men do—but I didn't ever remember being at a loss for words when presented with one.

It was only two weeks or so previous, when we'd been at that pretentious Hamptons party, where so many people were unkindly gossiping about her. And there she was that evening in her gallery, on the other side of a humiliation that would destroy a lesser person.

I could relate to what she was going through. I'd been there. It wasn't easy.

I'd known she was an exceptional woman, but I wasn't expecting what my eyes beheld that night. Her mass of jet-black hair was pulled into a messy ponytail, which, on anyone else, would have been overly sporty. But on her, it was the picture of elegance.

Of course it didn't hurt that I was also able to envision taking her hair down and burying my face it in.

Then, there was her dress, red crushed velvet with mini-sleeves—perhaps they were called cap sleeves?— and a button right at the throat. Just under that button was an opening, or maybe more accurately a *slit*, in the drapey fabric that opened nearly to her waistline.

The effect was mesmerizing with the dark red fabric against her pale skin. The opening revealed the tiniest sliver of inner breast, jiggling slightly when she walked. It pulled in at the waist with a belt and flared out again, swishing around her legs as she crossed the room.

Oh, mio dio.

But what really got me was the elegant way she carried herself, head held high but not so high she looked full of herself. That wasn't so easy to do when your personal life was all over the news.

"Gio!" Blu patted me on the back. "Lovely, isn't she?" he said, apparently having caught me staring. "Go say hi. I'm sure she'll be glad to see you."

"Blu, thank you. But I don't need anyone to push me to speak with a beautiful woman. I'm quite capable of doing it on my own."

Blu threw his hands in the air in surrender. "Okay, Gio. Calm down. Christ. Or *Cristo*. Whatever your people say."

He slunk off, too sensitive for his own good.

So I approached Avril. Which I was about to do, anyway, with or without Blu's urging.

"*Buona sera, mia cara.* I can't stop looking at you," I said when I finally had her to myself.

"Gio, thank you. It's good to see you again." She looked down, all modesty.

You had to love that, too. So many of these society wives—or in this case, ex-society wife—are so damn full of themselves, it's embarrassing. Like having access to your husband's millions makes you better than the next person? I think not.

In my life, I'd had access to nearly infinite riches and at other times had to scrape by, paycheck-to-paycheck. Neither situation had ever made me a better or worse person.

"Will you turn around for me so I can see your entire dress?" I asked.

She tilted her head at me and with a small smile, spun in her mile-high stilettos. And damn if that dress didn't have the same slit that exposed her back just like the one in the front.

"Stunning. Just stunning. Care to show me around?" I held my arm for her to take and let her lead the way.

While we walked, I wondered if she understood the full extent of the allegations against her husband. I figured she probably didn't, seeing as the nitty gritty details had yet to be made public and were known primarily only to people in the finance and investing world.

But her husband was in big trouble, and if he wasn't staying up at night worried about his future, he was a bigger idiot than I'd already thought for bailing on his gorgeous wife.

Avril hooked her arm in mine as we made our way through the maze of seating areas, tufted cushions, and floating curtains. The party was full of its usual suspects, good-looking men and women come together to express their sexuality.

It was odd to try to get to know her in such an unconventional setting, but nothing about my life had ever really been that normal, anyway. We walked past a couple going at it, moaning as loudly as I'd ever heard two people.

Just another day at the office.

"This is where I spend most of my day," Avril said, taking me into a very light room with white over-stuffed furniture, a glittery chandelier, and a huge glass desk.

"Wow. It's like a girl clubhouse."

She threw her head back and laughed, a sound I could easily get used to.

"I guess it is a little over-the-top girly, but I'd always wanted something like this, and it's the perfect contrast to the rest of the gallery."

And it suited her completely. We settled into the soft sofa.

"Cheers to you," I said, bringing my bourbon to her champagne.

"Thank you. Same to you."

"Well, you are doing a good service for Kink Lab, letting us hold our party here."

"I'm getting paid handsomely for it," she said.

"Is that the only reason you're doing it?" I asked, studying her. I had to know more about what made her tick.

"No, not exactly. But if I hadn't found a way to make the gallery profitable, I likely would have had to close it." She looked down at her drink. "Not a lot of galleries make money. They're often hobby businesses for those passionate about art."

"How did you get by before?" I asked.

"My husband made up the difference. But those days are over now."

"It looks to me like you are going to do just fine," I said. "Even better than fine. I'm guessing he cut you off?"

"He did. In so many ways. My driver was the last perk to go. My husband even suggested I get a car and start driving again—" She stopped short.

It was clear she'd spilled something she hadn't intended to. Did I dare ask?

"What about driving?"

"Ummm." She hesitated, such a sadness passing over her eyes that my chest tightened.

"I'll share my story if you share yours," I offered.

"Okay. You first," she said.

"All right. I grew up in *Milano*. Son of an importer, or so I thought."

She furrowed her beautiful brow. "What do you mean?" she asked.

"When I was about to leave for university, my father was arrested and sent to prison."

"Oh my god, Gio."

"The worst of it was that the rest of my family was in terrible danger. We had to flee Italy with little more than the clothes on our backs."

Her eyes widened, and she took my hand. "That's terrible."

"Turned out, he was an arms dealer and owed some bad guys a lot of money. We came to the U.S. under a special program and never looked back."

Those were sad days indeed, considering all that we left behind—most importantly, our father.

"So where is the rest of your family, now?" she asked.

"My mom passed away a few years after we arrived, pretty much of a broken heart. She didn't adjust well to the U.S., nor to life without my father. My three brothers live here in the States. We never saw our father again. He died in prison two years after we left Italy. Actually, I don't think his death was accidental, but nothing's ever been proven. When you have enemies like he did, anything is possible."

She looked at me, speechless, but I was used to that. The few people I shared my story with all looked at me like that when they first heard it.

"*Allora.* That's my story. Son of an arms dealer."

"Good god, Gio. You could write a book," she said

"I suppose I could. But I wouldn't. Every day, I try to forget that period of my life."

She nodded, her compassion bringing tears to my eyes.

"And you? You have a secret of your own?" I asked.

She took a deep breath. "Yeah. I don't drive, like I mentioned. The reason is that years ago, my sister died in a car accident when I was behind the wheel. I've never driven again."

I wanted to kiss the shame and sadness right off her face. "Oh, *cara.* I am so sorry." I took her hand and brushed my lips over the back of it.

"And my ex-husband insisting I start driving again is his evil way of twisting the knife in my heart. He knows I can't."

"What a horrible man. I have to tell you, darling—I've met him and know about his business dealings. You are far too good for him. You are better off without him, making your own new life."

She nodded. "I'm beginning to see that."

"*Cara,* do you mind if I kiss you?"

"First tell me what *cara* means."

I had to laugh at that. "It means *dear in* Italian. I'm sorry. Some habits die hard."

"No, it's okay. I like it. And I think I'd also like for you to kiss me."

Without waiting for me, she leaned forward until her lips met mine. Her kiss was as sweet as I knew it would be—soft and delicious, but confident and sexy as hell. No wonder the other guys all liked her.

I felt a twitch in my pants, the old boy waking right up, but this was not the time to pursue an amorous activity with this woman, regardless of the fact that we were right in the middle of a sex party. No, I wanted to be part of her new life, not some regret she left in the past with her ex.

"Darling, you know we are going to be seeing each other, yes?" I believed in getting right to the point.

"Well, Chase and Sumner mentioned they wanted to date me too, but that you all had some sort of *sharing* arrangement." She smiled and shook her beautiful head in disbelief, her black ponytail swishing around her puzzled face.

"I know. It's hard to understand at first. But while we guys are all different, we have often found ourselves falling for the same woman."

I probably shouldn't have said *falling*.

"Well," she said.

"Don't worry, *cara.* You will get used to the idea, and if it does not work for you, that is okay, too. We will always be your friends, and hopefully, your business partners. We want nothing but the best for you."

"Thank you, Gio. Thank you for being patient with me, and for listening to my story."

"My darling, you are more than welcome."

If all went according to my desires, I'd be hearing many more stories from my lovely Avril.

15

AVRIL

An arms dealer. Holy shit.

That was a first. I'd never known an arms dealer, nor anyone related to one. Not that I was aware of, anyway.

Now, I was kissing the son of one. Gio Rosselli, Italian stallion, tall with jet black hair and slightly crooked nose, whose English was peppered with just enough Italian to make a girl wet between her legs.

Oh my god. Did I just think that?

I never used to have a trashy mouth—until recently.

Also, until recently, I'd never kissed four different men who were friends and business partners. I hadn't been to a sex party, either—much less held one in my gallery.

I don't think every woman trying to build a new life

goes quite to the extremes I was, but sometimes, life dealt you a hand you had to play. And I wanted to play it hard.

But at the moment I was concentrating on Gio's whisper-soft kiss, which was building momentum. His lips gradually pressed harder on mine, and with such passion, it took my breath away.

My new dress, the one Juan had chosen for me at Barneys, and let me buy with Blu's fuck-buddy discount, was a hit. I hadn't been sure about wearing something with a slit from neck to waist, but when I tried it on, I could see that it was really discreet yet bold at the same time—a thrilling contrast.

I loved unexpected things, like having a girly office in a rough and tumble downtown loft.

And it turned out the opening in my dress served a purpose beyond just decorative. I guess a guy might call it *easy access*. Gio's fingers ran down the middle of the opening, causing my skin to explode in goose-bumps. He brushed just the insides of my breasts with his knuckles but went no further.

His other hand reached for mine, pressing it onto his trousers where his growing hard-on throbbed against my palm.

He pulled back, staring firmly into my eyes as he tightened my fingers around the girth of his cock.

Suddenly, he pushed my hand away.

"Lock the door," he demanded.

My breath caught.

But I pushed myself off the sofa and crossed to the door, praying that my trembling legs would carry me there and back.

I turned the lock just as he'd told me to. He had sunk into the sofa with an arm draped over the back, head tilted as he looked me up and down. I wasn't sure if he was trying to make me nervous, because in truth, he looked dark and even a little dangerous, especially after his arms dealer story. He opened his knees wide and pulled me into the space between them.

Sliding to the edge of the sofa until his face was just inches from my belly, he ran his hands up the sides of my dress, moving the fabric in small bunches as he pressed into the soft flesh of my thighs.

His touch was mesmerizing. I ran my fingers through his hair, gently raking his scalp with my nails, and he moaned, his eyes falling shut.

"God, you feel good, *cara*, and you smell so fine, too." He pressed his face into my belly and inhaled deeply.

I hoped he hadn't identified the scent of my excitement, but the truth was, he probably had. There was going to be no hiding it, especially since his hands had made their way under my dress and were heading for what Devon used to call *ground zero*.

Ugh. Why was that prick invading my thoughts? I was with one of the most beautiful, sexy men I'd ever laid eyes on. I shooed the creep away.

Fortunately, though, I didn't have to try too hard.

Gio lowered my panties, slowly and deliberately by reaching under my dress, until they were at my ankles. He raised one of my feet at a time so I could step out of them. He crumpled them into a ball, and finally meeting my gaze with an intensity that made me sway, smiled as he tucked them into his suit pocket.

Guess I won't be seeing those again.

His hands were under my dress again, lifting the slinky fabric until—well, until I was exposed.

I hadn't been with a man besides my husband in so long—aside from kissing the other guys—that I almost shrank away in modesty.

"*Cara*, are you all right?" Gio asked.

That was a good question. *Was* I all right? I wasn't so sure.

But I wanted to be. "Yeah. Yes. I am," I muttered, nodding.

When my dress was high enough and Gio was face to face with my bare skin, he leaned in for a deep inhale. Closing his eyes in satisfaction, he murmured, "Your pussy smells beautiful, just like I knew it would."

Pussy. I used to think that word was vulgar. I'd never used it and didn't think I ever would. But Gio made me feel so desired and beautiful that it took on a softer meaning.

And what the hell. It was just a word.

"Ahh, so soft and smooth," he whispered, running his fingers over my bare lips.

I had to hold his shoulders if I wanted to remain standing.

He took another inhale and spread me open with his thumbs, just the tiniest bit. His tongue flicked my clit, which was erect by then and very sensitive. I was growing wetter by the moment and wondered if I might just gush all over him.

"Your pussy tastes so good, *cara*. Mmmm," he moaned.

I widened my stance instinctively, his palm sweeping between my legs, coming back with evidence of my excitement. He pulled his hand to his face and took another deep inhale.

Next thing I knew, he was standing. He turned me until my back faced the sofa, and he lowered me to sitting. Kneeling, he reached under my knees and pulled me forward until my ass rested on the edge of the sofa and my pussy was at the perfect level for his attentions.

His finger ventured along my slit, from top to bottom, pausing to spread my wetness along my sensitive folds.

I whimpered involuntarily when his tongue returned to my sex, his thumb paused at my opening. My breath came hard, and my heartbeat raced. I knew I was on the verge of an orgasm, and he'd really only just gotten started.

But I'd not been with someone like Gio—or Ash or

Chase or Sumner—ever in my life. They were strong, confident, and thoughtful men.

If that wasn't a turn-on, I didn't know what was.

And my orgasm was closer than I'd even realized. In one swift motion, Gio had entered me with two fingers at the same time his lips encircled my clit. They formed a suction that hurled me over my edge. The room filled with screams before I realized they were my own.

Christ, what I'd been missing.

He continued to piston my pussy until another orgasm rocked me. I had to squeeze the sofa cushions for purchase, and my head thrashed back and forth.

As he slowed, my thighs shook violently. I tried to still them with my hands, but it didn't help. After he'd rained kisses down the insides of my legs, he gently drew my knees together and crawled up on the sofa, cradling my shivering, wasted body.

He stroked my now-messy ponytail. "*Cara*, you are so beautiful, please tell me you'll spend more time with me and the other guys."

"I—I don't know Gio." I snuggled into his long arms.

"What is it that has you worried?"

"I'm not sure I want to be shared. I may want just one partner." I sat up so I could face him and smoothed out my dress. God, he was gorgeous.

I continued, "The most important thing is that I don't end up with another asshole like my soon-to-be-ex."

He gave a small laugh.

Someone on the other side of my door yanked on the knob. "Av? Av, you in there?" a voice hollered.

"Shit. That's Blu," I said, jumping up and rearranging my dress.

"*Cara*," Gio said, "you have nothing to hide. He knows how we feel about you."

I guess he did.

I pulled the door open as I tucked lose hairs back into my ponytail holder. Blu looked from me to Gio.

"Oh. Okay. I hadn't seen you in awhile," he said.

I stepped out of my office to look around at the party.

Sex.

There was sex everywhere.

As there should have been. It was a sex party, after all.

16

ASH

THE FIRST KINK LAB HELD AT AVRIL'S GALLERY WAS A massive success.

It was clear she'd gone into the venture with a lot of trepidation, but the party came off without a hitch, and Avril's bank account was about to be richer by one hundred thousand dollars.

A great night all around, if you asked me.

And damn, if she wasn't drop-dead gorgeous at the party. Gio, the lucky bastard, got her all to himself and was now seriously love struck.

I was right behind him with my turn. I was picking her up at the school for special kids, where she taught art, and then we were going to get something to eat and listen to jazz.

My cab dropped me where Avril did her volunteering. It looked like any other elementary school, with hand-drawn pictures in the windows and monkey bars over a huge sand pit.

After I was buzzed inside, I ducked my head into what I guessed was the school's office.

"I'm looking for Avril Crane," I said to the white-haired lady behind the counter.

"Oh, yes. One moment please. " She flipped through some papers. "Ash? Ash Singh?"

"Yes that's me."

"She told me she was expecting you. She's in the third classroom on the right, if you'd like to go take a peek."

School office workers hadn't changed much since I was last in the elementary grades in New Jersey.

I took my time wandering down the hall, amazed at both the familiarity and the strangeness of the elementary school where everything was designed to suit the height of four-foot tall mini-humans.

The place smelled vaguely of paste and dusty books, and cork bulletin boards were crowded with large stenciled letters reminding people to have a good day. There was a quiet buzz as adult voices floated out of the classrooms, followed by a chorus of children's' voices.

It was all so sweet, it made me forget for one moment what I'd hoped to do with Avril later that night.

When I found her class, I stood in the doorway

where I could watch her in action. She buzzed around the room with an apron over her clothes, helping her little students with their masterpieces. She was so in her element, laughing and encouraging her charges, hard at work at their tiny desks and chairs.

Finally, I caught her eye.

She moved from the crouched position where she was talking to an unhappy little artist crying over, from what I could see, a disagreement about who got to use the green paint next. Smoothing out her apron, she headed over to me.

"Hi! I'm so sorry. I lost track of time. Let me gather my things."

"Hey," I said. I grabbed her hand and pulled her into the empty hallway.

"What's wrong?" she asked, her eyes wide.

Fuck, she was a beauty.

I leaned close to her, so closely, I could smell what I guessed was simple shampoo and a small spritz of Chanel. Bringing my finger to her cheek, I said, "You have a little smudge of paint right here on your cheek."

Her hand flew to her face. "Oh, I do? Where? Here?"

"I've got it," I whispered, pushing her hand out of the way.

Just as I'd gotten it nearly off, I heard a sound behind us. Two little artists from the class were peeking out the door at us.

"Well, hello," I said to the spies.

They giggled. "Are you her husband?" one of them asked.

I shook my head. "No, I am not."

"Are you her boyfriend, then?" Something about the line of questioning struck them as funny. They ran away in a fit of giggles, screaming, "Miss Avril has a boy. He's over there."

I never would have guessed I'd be so completely intimidated by a bunch of six-year-olds. "Hey, let's get out of here before they trap us and pin us down."

She burst out laughing. "Give me one minute to wash my hands and grab my purse."

While Avril did her thing, I stood in the doorway again. Every six-year-old in the room stared me down. They were clearly a little protective of their Miss Avril. Just like we four guys were.

WE SETTLED into our table at the cozy, dark jazz club I'd chosen and ordered a couple martinis.

Avril took a sip of hers, first. "Ahhh. Just what the doctor ordered. I so need this. And just what one should drink when at a jazz club. Cheers," she said, raising her glass.

"You were so great with those kids. I loved watching you."

It was hard to tell in the dim light, but I could swear

she blushed just the tiniest amount. *I loved a modest woman.*

"They're great. I just adore them," she said. "I'm so lucky I get to work with them. It's been such a great thing to look forward to." She stared thoughtfully into her martini glass as the music started.

"Avril, speaking of this time in your life, I wanted to talk to you about your ex-husband."

"Really? Well, he's my soon-to-be ex. We're meeting with lawyers tomorrow."

"Okay, good. Then what I'm going to tell you is more important than I'd thought."

She furrowed her brow with a *what the hell are you talking about* look.

"Devon's alleged to have committed some serious crimes. Avril, I don't know how much you know about this, but you are very, very lucky you two split up. You could have been considered an accomplice. Spouses are often in on the husbands' misdeeds."

"*WHAT?*" she said, nearly slopping the contents of her martini out of its glass.

"You know he's under investigation, right?" I asked.

"Yes, but Chase, he told me high profile people are under investigation all the time."

Of course he said that. He was an asshole.

"Well, that's partly true. But in his case, the investigation was warranted. He has potentially engaged in insider trading and also in defrauding clients. He'll probably be going before a grand jury very soon."

Her hand flew to her mouth. "Oh my god. And it was probably going on right under my nose. I hate that man." She rubbed her forehead.

"Hey, hey. This will all be behind you some day." I reached for her hands.

She shook her head. "Wow. Just wow. How it is that you know this?"

"We work in the same circles. There are no secrets. Only rumors, lies, and the cold hard truth. And this one turned out to be the truth."

She pursed her lips then looked at me with wide eyes, absentmindedly flipping the ends of her long hair.

"Hey. Want to get out of here?" I asked.

"Yeah. Yes, please."

"Where do you want to go?"

She stood. "My place?"

Who was I to argue with that?

AVRIL'S PENTHOUSE apartment was everything I'd thought it would be. I mean, I had a nice place, and it was just a few blocks away from hers, but this one was freaking palatial. It was filled with lots of old world architectural details but decorated with the kind of modern art only a gallery owner would have an eye for. The effect was stunning.

Like Avril.

Her heels clicked over the marble floors, but before we got halfway down her huge foyer, I took her hand and pushed her up against the wall.

"I can't help myself," I breathed, running my hand over her silky black hair. "I've been dying to kiss you since I wiped that paint off your face."

She gave me a shy smile. "Then what the hell are you waiting for?"

I grabbed a fistful of her hair and tilted her head until her neck was exposed. Running my lips from her collarbone to her earlobe, I feasted on her sweet skin.

My hands ran down her back until they landed on her ass, where I filled my happy mitts with fistfuls of her fleshy behind.

"Angel," I said, "where's the bedroom?"

"Mmmm. This way. Come with me," she said, throwing a look over her shoulder.

When we reached her room, I wasted no time in lifting her dress over her head. There she stood before me, in nothing more than matching lace bra and thong.

I stepped back to take it all in. Yeah, she was one fucking amazing beauty.

Her breasts nearly flowed over the cups of her bra, and the smooth, flawless skin of her stomach led the way to some of the most gorgeous lace I'd ever seen. I could only imagine what lie beneath.

SHE GRASPED my cock through my trousers and damn if I didn't almost shoot my load right then. That's how hot I was. Seriously worked up.

I kicked off my shoes and flung my suit jacket aside. Avril made quick work of my shirt buttons, and I opened my trousers and let them and my boxers fall to the floor. As soon as I was free, she moved for my hard-on, stroking me with determination.

She was hungry for release, just like I was. The only thing that would wash away the intensity of her emotions—and mine, too—was a physical experience of epic proportions.

And I was ready to give her just that.

17

AVRIL

No one had ever called me angel. A month of firsts.

Ash stood before me, gloriously naked with a brutally hard cock, which was heavy as hell and throbbing in my hand.

I stroked him in slow motion, enjoying the velvet of his brown skin. When I reached the head of his erection, I had to loosen my grip to fit over its swelling. A glistening drop of precum hung from his tip. I swiped at it with my forefinger and brought it to my mouth to taste.

But before I did, I made sure he was looking at me. I wanted him to know I was relishing him and everything about him.

"Yeah, baby, taste my cum," he growled as my finger entered my mouth.

It was sweet and salty, just like I knew it would be.

"You like it?" he asked.

My gaze was locked with his as I nodded, *yes*.

"Turn around," he demanded.

I did as he said and faced my bed. I didn't know what he was up to, but whatever it was, I could pretty much guarantee it would be earth shattering. He was just that kind of guy.

With my back to him, he now had perfect access to my bra clasp, which he quickly unhooked. His hands flew to my breasts, by now aching for his attention. As if he knew just what I needed, he pulled my nipples until I whimpered. It was a good thing I was standing just before the bed, because I was not at all sure how long I'd be able to remain upright on my feet.

He pushed my hair forward and over my shoulders, leaving the bare skin of my back uncovered for his lips.

His hands smoothed over my belly, then returned to the cheeks of my ass. He stroked them so lightly that I was moments from losing my mind. After a small nibble on the back of my neck, he hooked his fingers in the lace of my thong and pulled it to the floor where I stepped out of it and kicked it aside. He remained crouched behind me, his face level with my ass.

"Bend forward," he said, his hand on my lower back, gently directing me.

Was he serious? My behind would be right in his face.

Oh. Maybe that was the point.

I leaned onto the bed to support myself in a ninety-degree angle. Ash's warm breath traveled up the crack of my behind, and I squirmed from the sensation. My legs quivered, and my breaths came long and deep.

"Reach back here," he said.

Really?

I put my hands on the cheeks of my ass. What was he getting at?

"Open yourself for me, baby," he murmured.

No, no, no. Don't think so.

"You're beautiful, Avril. Let me see all of you."

Oh. God.

Ugh. I squeezed my eyes closed in shame, and pressed my fingers lightly into the cheeks of my ass.

"Yeah. Like that. Now give me a bit more."

Okay, now would be a good time to die.

But no such luck.

I pulled a bit more on my cheeks, hoping this would satisfy his dirty curiosity about my most private parts.

Why didn't he just lay me on my back and crawl up between my legs, like normal men did?

Or was everyone doing this, now? It was like there was this party going on that I was finally invited to.

And I was accepting the invitation.

Opening myself further, much to Ash's delight, gave him the space he needed to reach for the wetness between my legs. I pushed back a bit against him because I just couldn't help it. I didn't know what he intended to give me, but I was quite sure I was going to like it.

I took a deep breath. "Ash. Will you fuck me? Please."

I'd never thought those words before that night, much less muttered them out loud. But I felt so safe in Ash's worship. I wanted to feel him inside me, filling me up, stroking me hard.

He turned me back to face him and laid his lips on mine with a desperate ferocity. I ran my hands over his nipples and down his muscular abs until I reached his cock once again. I pulled back to watch his pleasure, and his eyes fell shut. He sucked his breath in a harsh gasp as I ran my fingers over his balls, leaving a trail of goosebumps behind.

I stood a little taller, satisfied with my feminine prowess.

I swayed for a moment, and he caught me, his eyes having snapped open into pools of deep, dark brown. He backed me up to the bed, lowering me onto it and reaching for his trousers at the same time. He came back with a condom.

When he was done rolling it over his long erection, he touched between my legs, cupping my sex.

"You're so goddamn wet, angel," he growled.

By now, I was weak with desire, ready to beg him for whatever he could give me. Yeah, I'd been with his friends just days before, but at that moment in time, we were the only two people in the world.

And that was fine by me.

He notched the head of his cock in my slit, sliding it around for a second until he found my opening. I gave way to an inch of him, when he stopped.

"You okay?"

I loved that he checked in.

I could only nod and whisper, "Yes, yes, yes…"

He paused, then drove deep inside me, leaving me screaming from the intensity.

Over the sound of my own moans, I heard him growl my name. He tunneled inside me one more time and held himself there while an orgasm hit me like a truck. My back arched as if I could actually take more of him, and my arms flailed on the disheveled bed, trying to find purchase in the sheets. He pistoned me through another climax and quickly joined me in his own with a violent shudder and long, loud roar.

Hi forehead dropped onto mine, our eyes so close, we couldn't even see each other.

That was okay, though. He was burned into my memory.

THE NEXT DAY was going to be an unforgettable one.

I was floating, thanks to the hotter than hot night

I'd had with Ash, a feeling I was struggling to hold on to with everything I had.

And I was now sitting with my lawyer in a fancy conference room that I was sure was being paid for, in part, by the huge fees he was charging me. We were waiting for Devon and his attorney.

The door flew open, and an admin showed them in. But Devon and his lawyer had not come alone.

No. They'd also brought Dagney, my former assistant.

Speechless. That's what I was.

My lawyer spoke up. "May I ask who you've brought along with you here, Mr. Crane?"

Clearly oblivious to the gravity of his dick move, Devon smiled brightly.

"Oh, this is Dagney Gardner. My fiancée."

What. The. Actual. Fuck.

"You two are getting married?" I asked.

My lawyer patted me on the arm in an attempt to quiet me, but it did no good.

I popped to my feet and leaned over the conference room table. "How the *hell* are you getting married? We're not even divorced yet."

They were all taken aback by my ferocity.

How did I ever love this fucking asshole? And how had I ever thought he was handsome? He was now the ugliest piece of shit I'd ever laid my eyes on.

"Now calm down, Av. That's just a technicality. Of course we aren't getting married until you and I are—"

He looked around the room, as if realizing a bit too late that maybe he should have kept his big goddamn mouth shut.

"Okay, let's all remain calm," Devon's attorney said. "Mrs. Crane, let's sit down again, shall we?"

I was sure I didn't owe it to my husband's attorney to return to my seat, but I did it anyway. None of us wanted the meeting to drag on any longer than necessary.

But I did take the opportunity to rake my eyes over Dagney.

She was clearly enjoying an upgrade in her wardrobe, and wouldn't you know it, she was wearing the goddamn necklace I'd found in Devon's coat pocket—the one I had assumed was for me, because who the hell else was my loving husband going to give an expensive piece of jewelry to, for fuck's sake?

What a fool I'd been.

The meeting commenced, but I was so overcome with hatred for Devon and Dagney that I barely followed it until he started making noises about a car. Again.

"Yes, I agree to get her a car since she won't have a driver anymore," he said.

That did it. "Look, you asshole. You know I don't drive. Stop dangling that in front of me. Haven't you already done the damage you wanted to?"

Dagney rolled her eyes. If she did that one more

time, she wouldn't be leaving the room with her eyesight.

"Now let's not get excited—" my lawyer started to say.

But I cut him off. "Devon, don't be smug with me. Everyone in this room here, with the possible exception of your whore over there, is aware that you are probably facing prison time."

Dagney's face lost all its color. Protectively, her fingers flew to the necklace I'd thought was intended for me. If her relationship went to shit, it was all she'd walk away with.

Except for my disgust with her.

But Devon's face was just as pale. "How did you know?" he asked, his voice trailing off.

"EVERYBODY knows, Devon. You're over. Finished. And I'm getting out of this marriage just in time to let you enjoy your little shitshow all by yourself. Well, except for Dagney, who's probably gonna bail right after this meeting."

Bile rose in my throat, and I was shaking with rage. I was just as angry with myself as at anyone else in the room, for being a fool to believe I was living anything other than a superficial existence surrounded by opportunistic people and a husband who'd leave me for my assistant.

I felt the tears coming, and I wasn't about to give Devon the satisfaction of seeing me upset. I turned to my lawyers.

"Do what you have to do. I'm leaving."

"But Mrs. Crane—" someone called after me.

I got through the door just in time to stifle my first sob. I ran for the elevator past the staring receptionist who, to be honest, probably saw shit like mine all the time.

It wasn't until I was in the elevator and had pressed the *down* button that I finally let loose.

Something had died and taken a big piece of me with it.

But I'd been through this before. I could endure.

There was really no choice, was there?

18

SUMNER

Chase and Gio were already in the conference room for our founders' meeting when I arrived.

I took my usual seat, facing the large window that overlooked the offices of some news magazine, while we waited for Ash.

Smith poked his head through the door. "You guys having a meeting without me?" he asked.

"Sorry, Smith," I said, "this is for us guys only."

He rolled his eyes and stormed off.

"In my country, we would call that guy a *stronzo*," Gio said, shaking his head.

"I don't know what that means, but I'm pretty sure I agree with you," I said.

"I'm with you, Sum. He annoys the hell out of me," Chase said. "Even if he does do good work."

He was right, and we all nodded in agreement. Smith was brilliant with the numbers and had found us many successful ventures we never would have pursued without his in-depth analysis.

Too bad he had the maturity of a teenage boy. It was why he wasn't part of Kink Lab.

And of course, he knew nothing about the special proclivities of the rest of us. Best to keep that sort of thing away from an immature big mouth, no matter how gifted he was.

Not that we were ashamed of our arrangements. But New York, and the circles we traveled in, could be strangely insular. We'd 'come out' someday, but the time hadn't been right just yet.

Ash came running in, sweat dripping from his brow.

"Guys, sorry." He poured himself a glass of water, which he immediately chugged.

"You just getting in?" I asked. "It's noon, buddy."

"Yeah. Shit." He straightened his tie and pulled his jacket closed to cover his wrinkled shirt. "Sorry guys. Let's start."

His was a serious *walk of shame* if I'd ever seen one, but if he didn't want to talk about it that was fine by me. We all knew he'd had an evening with the lovely Avril, and we were happy for him. And actually, happier that he'd been late for work, coming in only half put-together.

It told us all they'd had a great time.

And didn't that bode well for the rest of us?

We went over our quarterly numbers and discussed the work we had on the table. Our business was growing and our universe expanding. We'd begun looking at deals in Hong Kong and Belgium.

I wouldn't have minded a little international travel. Perhaps I could encourage Avril to join me…

"Hey! Earth to Sumner," Chase said.

"Sorry, guys. My mind wandered."

"Uh, gee. Wonder where it went?" Chase wore a shit-eating grin on his face.

"Perhaps this is a good time to talk about the elephant in the room," Gio said.

"And which elephant would that be, Gio?" Ash asked.

"Why don't you tell us, Ash, with your wrinkled shirt and crooked tie?"

"All right, all right, guys. How's everyone feeling about Avril?" I asked. Somebody had to have some balls.

We all looked at Ash.

He nodded slowly, with a look in his eyes I'd never seen. "Yeah, man. She's amazing. I want to date her. That's all there is to it. What about the rest of you?"

We all looked from one to the other for a quick moment.

"I'm in. In fact, I'm seeing her tonight," I said.

"Go Sumner," Ash said with a smile.

And Gio and Chase nodded in agreement.

"She'll need time. But she seems open to dating us. All of us," Ash added.

THE REST of the day dragged by, and I found myself watching the clock until it was time to pick up Avril. The guys had noticed I wasn't completely there as well, but they didn't say anything. They knew how it was, and if our beautiful girl consented, I supposed they'd be next.

Smitten, that's what we were.

Our girl. If that wasn't jumping the gun, I didn't know what was. But I didn't care.

Avril had texted me she was running a bit late, so I wandered around Soho until I found a bar to grab a drink in. I ordered a beer and sent a text to my mom in Italy. It would be late there, but she might still be up.

Hey Mom

Sweetie!

How's the trip?

Wonderful. Just wonderful. We're in this little town called Padova. It's where Romeo and Juliet come from. Or someone like that

Sounds great, Mom

Saw some nice linen shirts in a shop, made right on the premises. Would you like one?

Sure, I'd love one. Get an XL. I'm big by Italian standards

Okay sweetie. Going to bed now. Got an early morning with the girls

Love you Mom

Love you too, honey xoxox

Ah, Mom. She wasn't perfect by any measure, but she'd held us together after my dad had bailed. And she's the one who came out on top, if you ask me. She had a great life with great friends and was always busy. In fact, she was *so* busy, I had a hard time pinning her down for an occasional meal together.

But I couldn't be happier for her. She'd never met another guy after Dad, and I didn't blame her for staying single. With the way he fucked her over, if it were me, I'd never want another man in my life, either.

So I cherished spoiling the hell out of her, treating her to trips and other activities. One of the benefits of all my hard work.

I could think of someone else I'd like to spoil...if she'd give me the chance. Speaking of which...

Hi, Sum, just wrapping things up

Super. Be there in ten

I finished up my beer and glanced up at the TV playing in the corner of the bar. Wouldn't you know, my shithead father was being interviewed on CNN, talking out of his ass like he always did.

"Senator Larlaith..." the star struck reporter began.

I threw some money on the bar and turned to leave.

I didn't need him to ruin my night, even if he did seem to be nearly everywhere I went.

BY THE TIME I got to Avril's, I'd forgotten my irritation over seeing the good senator on TV. I'd managed to push it out of my mind, preferring to think of my mother having fun in Italy and how much I was looking forward to seeing my lovely girl.

I rang the bell to the place where Kink Lab had been held just a couple nights before. In the daylight, the heavy front door looked so innocent and utilitarian. But after dark, it promised sensual adventures of all kinds. Blu had done a good job recruiting Avril, or should I say, her gallery?

"Hey, gorgeous," I said, pulling her to me by the waist.

She felt slim and firm, and her silky black hair tickled the arm I'd hooked around her.

"Mmmm," she said after a sexy-as-hell kiss. She leaned back to meet my gaze. "Hey, are you okay?"

"Yeah, just saw my father on TV. An ugly reminder. He bailed on me and my mom a long time ago."

"I'd heard you were a senator's son. Now I know why you don't talk about it. I'm sorry."

I burrowed my nose into her hair, which smelled clean and spicy, like the fancy shampoo they used where I got my hair cut. I could get used to that soothing scent.

"I was wondering if you'd like to have dinner here?" she asked.

"Here? In the studio?"

"Yeah. I could get something delivered. I've got adult beverages."

She looked so excited at the prospect of "staying in," that I couldn't say no. And I was a big fan of the gallery —for obvious reasons—anyway.

"Let's get some wine," she said, taking my hand and leading me to a little seating area in the corner of the large space.

I looked around the gallery in wonderment. "Sure looks different from the other night, doesn't it?" I asked.

"Totally. It was so amazing how your workers set the place up and broke it down so quickly. Just a couple hours after the last guest left, you'd never know a thing had gone on here. Like the party disappeared without a trace." She shrugged at the mystery.

"I didn't see you much that night," I teased.

And wouldn't you know, she blushed. I liked that.

"Well...that's true..." she stumbled.

I took a sip of the delicious wine she'd poured and settled back on the sofa.

"Sweetie, I'm just teasing you. I know you were playing with Gio, and I think that's great. I fully support it."

And it was true. I loved that they'd gotten together. And that she'd been with Ash the night before, and Chase several days before.

Or something like that. I couldn't keep track. She probably couldn't, either.

She opened her mouth to say something, but stopped, like she didn't know *what* the hell to say.

"Hey," I said, reaching for her hand. "It's okay. The four of us guys are all about this shit. You know that."

She took a deep breath, and her shoulders relaxed. Setting her wine glass on the table in front of us, she scooted closer. With her fingers running through my hair, she brought her lips to mine. Her mouth was soft and open, ready for me like a ripe peach.

She pulled back and looked at me with a sly smile.

"I'm not starving. Can you wait a while before we eat?"

Actually, I *was* starving. But I was more hungry for her. Hell, I'd wait a thousand years if it meant I could kiss her.

"Nope, I'm good. I don't need anything."

Thinking with the little head, as the guys called it. But hey, we *all* did that from time to time.

I put my hands on either side of her beautiful face. "I could look at you all day long," I whispered.

She looked down, modest as ever. "Follow me," she said, extending her hand.

I grabbed my wine and did as I was told.

19

AVRIL

Fortunately, Sumner was not hungry for dinner, which meant we could have a little fun before ordering.

I had to admit, I'd been thinking about him all day, in spite of the fact that I'd been with Ash just before.

What a little slut I was turning into.

Before he'd arrived at the gallery, I'd had time for a brief chat with Blu.

"Honey, I'm so glad you're getting some from *real* men. Unlike that douchebag ex of yours," he said.

I really didn't want to think of Devon right then, especially since he'd taken every opportunity he could to mutilate my soul. The fucker.

"It's all pretty incredible," I said.

"Listen to my girl, all happy and shit."

I guess being Blu's 'project' wasn't the worst thing in the world. I mean, I was pretty much coming out on top in every regard, in spite of being screwed over by my husband and assistant.

Happiness is the best revenge, they said. And I was pretty sure I was on the right track. But there was one thing nagging at me, a little reminder sitting on my shoulder and pecking away at me every time I got too happy.

"But Blu, there is, um, one thing."

"What's that darlin'?" He was typing furiously in the background, probably arranging his evening's hook up. "Shit, I wish more of these guys would send dick pics. How the hell am I supposed to choose?"

"Too much information, Blu. Thanks, anyway."

"Sorry, Av. Got carried away. What's on your mind? I have closed my laptop, and you have my undivided attention." I heard the telltale *click* in the background.

"Well, I am not sure about dating all these guys. I mean, in the end, I really only want one. At least, I think so."

"Are you nuts? You know how many girls would love to have a man harem, especially with those four guys you're fucking—"

"I'm not fucking them, Blue." Well, not *all* of them, anyway.

"Oh, sweetie, don't get technical with me. But look. Do you have to choose? I mean, what's wrong with being with all of them? I've known these guys a long time. They're more than decent. I wish they were gay, but that's my cross to bear."

Was he still bitter about that?

"I cannot be with four men. That's ludicrous," I said.

"All right. Suit yourself, ya prude." He sighed dramatically.

Okayyy...

And now, in my gallery, I was face-to-face with one of the four amazing men who'd stumbled into my life—the stunning and dimpled Sumner Larlaith, U.S. senator's son. How the hell I was going to choose one guy? Or could I manage all four? That was, if they even wanted me?

Were they a package deal? Were the choices all or none?

I'd have to worry about that later. At the moment, I just wanted to focus on Sumner.

There was something about him that had struck me the first time I'd laid eyes on him. I blushed when he looked my way, like a shy teenager. I couldn't put my finger on why, but it was as if when he looked at me, he really *saw* me.

I took him by the hand and led him to the middle of the gallery, which had been ground zero for all things naughty when the Kink Lab party had been in full swing.

With the usual furniture returned to its normal

place, the room was now anchored by a medium-sized conference table surrounded by eight chairs. I pushed Sumner up against the table's edge until his ass was resting on it, and wedged myself between his legs.

With my hands holding his face, I pressed my forehead to his and took a deep inhale of his delicious scent, some sort of combination of plain soap and clean, masculine skin.

God, I could get used to that.

Angling my head back, he kissed the top of my nose, a touch so tender and intimate a lump rose in my throat. His lips wandered to my mouth for a sumptuous kiss. I was so spellbound, I'd barely realized that he'd unbuttoned my blouse until his hands cupped my breasts, the lace of my white bra sliding down to expose heated skin.

I wanted to not think of anything, and we were headed in the perfect direction for just that.

Sumner thumbed my hard, aching nipples, and even more so when I arched my back to give more of myself.

I shrugged my blouse off my shoulders until it fluttered to the floor, then reached to unhook my bra. When my breasts were fully exposed, he lowered his mouth to them and tormented me with licks and nibbles. My head dropped back, my hair swinging behind me and brushing my waist, reminding me I had a skirt and panties to remove.

But before I could, Sumner was on the job, unzipping me and then hooking his fingers in my thong to push my clothes below my ass. I wriggled the rest of the way out of them and fumbled for his belt and fly, eager to get into his pants. We'd never been naked together before then, having kissed only briefly the night he brought me home from the first Kink Lab I'd attended.

And our coming together felt as natural as anything ever had for me—certainly more natural than the first, awkward time I'd been with Devon.

"Baby, you're so beautiful," Sumner said, looking me up and down. His words melted me, and at that moment, I would have done anything for him. He slipped off the conference table to finish removing his clothes.

And lord, if he wasn't beautiful himself, wearing nothing more than his birthday suit.

He lowered me to the sheepskin rug in front of the gallery's decorative fireplace and spread my legs apart. Positioning himself between them, his hands smoothed over my feverish skin.

I writhed under him, and we'd only just gotten started.

He pushed my breasts together, kissing them, then moving his lips down my abdomen. They brushed across my belly, leaving me quivering and exploding in goosebumps.

He traveled lower still, toward my aching sex. When

he got close enough, his warm breath brushed over me before he actually touched me. I was wild with desire and frantic for release.

And just when I thought I'd lose my mind, his tongue traveled the length of my slit, parting my lips to get to my soaked core. His finger teased at my opening and slowly worked its way in, making a *come here* motion that had me screaming in a matter of seconds.

My head rolled back and forth over the sheepskin, and I wove my fingers into his hair, taking fistfuls and pulling hard to release the tension from my drawn-out orgasm.

"Goddamn, your pussy tastes good."

He moved to zero in on my clit, his lips forming a perfect suction around my hard little nub.

"God, Sumner. That feels so nice…" I murmured, just as I was shattered by another orgasm.

He slowed his attentions, moaning lightly. I raised my head to see his hard cock in his hand, moving with slow strokes as he pulled back from my still-throbbing pussy.

"I'm getting a condom, baby," he said, turning to reach for the trousers that lay on the floor in the puddle of our clothing.

My hands flew to my sensitive clit, and while I watched him unroll the condom over his brutally hard cock, I made light circles. My entire sex was soaked with my juices.

I was ready for him and his thick erection.

He positioned my knees over his shoulders and aimed his cock at the notch of my opening. I gasped as he entered an inch, opening me slowly, in preparation for all of him.

He pushed further. "You okay, baby?"

"Yeah...give it to me. Fuck me, Sumner," I whimpered.

It was inconceivable that, even though I'd already come twice, I needed more. I needed *him*.

So he drove into me until he was balls-deep and pulled back out, pistoning with a fury that left us both breathless, him moaning, and me screaming. His orgasm, marked by a growl that grew louder and louder, sparked mine. This time, I felt a satisfaction that was complete.

I was whole, and strong, and femininely powerful.

"God, baby, I'm coming," he murmured.

I watched him, his eyes closed and face tense, grinding his teeth until the urge to explode was satisfied. His pumping slowed as his face relaxed and his eyes opened, gazing down at me.

"You are fucking amazing," he said, kissing me on the forehead.

He lay next to me on the rug and pulled me into his arms. Our legs entwined, and I buried my head in his chest, lightly damp with perspiration from our exertion.

I looked up at him. "That was incredible. So yummy."

He laughed. "Maybe we could do it again some day."

"Well, I was thinking the same thing, but you know, I don't want to wear you out."

"Ha. That'll never happen. But I might wear *you* out."

"Hmmm," I said. "We'll just have to see about that."

20

CHASE

Shortly after that article in the *New York Post* had come out, the one about the RESLR team, Ruby's nanny told me there'd been several hang-up calls on my landline.

I thought nothing of it since solicitation calls were endemic, but about the fifth time she mentioned it, I started to wonder what the hell was going on.

Turned out I didn't have to wait long for my answer.

While I normally let calls to my landline go to voicemail, I took a chance on picking up the phone while waiting for Avril to come over. She'd wanted to meet Ruby, and I wanted to spend more time with her. Perfect way to see both my girls at once.

Oof. Did I really just say 'my girls?'

I reached for the phone on the fifth ring, just before voicemail picked up.

"Hello."

Nothing.

"Hello?"

I waited for a moment, and then a woman's voice came in, faint but also familiar.

"Chase?"

"Hello? Yes this is Chase. Could you please speak up?" I asked.

"Chase, it's me."

Who was *me*?

"Excuse me? Can you tell me who this is?"

"Minette."

Had someone just punched me in the gut? Because it sure felt like it.

"Chase? Are you still there?"

I had to fight the urge to throw the phone through the wall. I didn't want to wake Ruby.

Plus, I really didn't want a hole in my wall.

"Uh, yeah. I'm here"

"It's been awhile, Chase."

I pictured her long brown hair and how it swung in the wind when she walked. Wait. Stop. I didn't want to have any happy memories of her.

"Yeah, it has been a while, Minette. What do you want?" I was trying to be as nice as I could. I didn't feel too hopeful about that, though.

"I've missed you, Chase."

"Gee, thanks for calling to tell me that. What about your daughter, Ruby? Do you miss her?" My daughter's mother didn't bring out the best in me. *Down boy.* Getting worked up over this was not going to help anyone.

"Of course I miss my baby. I want to come see you. Both of you."

My stomach churned again. "Not a good idea, Minette. And I gotta run. Next time send a postcard—"

"Chase, wait…"

I'd never heard her plead before. "Minette, why did you call? Do you need something? I thought things were going well at the ballet."

"They are. They really are. I got a solo for the upcoming season. It's just that I saw the article about you in the New York Post, and I began realizing I made a mistake leaving you and Ruby."

There it was, transparent as glass. She'd found I was not only making good money but serious fucking money, the kind a dancer for the city ballet would never see. That is, unless she married it.

And now she wanted to be a mom to Ruby? And a partner to me?

I had to admit, for a moment, I was tempted to say *yes* if it would clean up the inevitable mess she'd left behind.

My heart broke on a pretty much regular basis for my baby Ruby, who would one day find out her mother walked without looking back. I knew when that day came, my little girl would be left full of questions—and heartache.

Until then, it was my job to protect her as best I could, and that included keeping the very woman who'd given up her baby for no other reason than 'she didn't feel like a mother' at arm's reach.

"Minette, you left Ruby and me. At first, it was hard. But now we're okay. You're not welcome back in our lives. I'm sorry."

I felt like bastard for taking such a hard line, but my first priority was my daughter. That's all there was to it.

I TOOK a deep breath to shake off the negative conversation with Minette, and was about to peek in on Ruby, when the door buzzer rang.

My heart skipped a beat knowing Avril was on her way up. I pulled the baby's door closed so we wouldn't wake her and went to open the door for my beautiful guest.

And what a beauty she was. I'd never seen her dressed casually, and boy, did she pull it off. With her slim capri pants and little flats, she looked like she'd stepped out of an Audrey Hepburn movie. She had her hair twisted into a long braid that hung over the front of her right shoulder, which was bare thanks to a little halter top that showed off her flawless skin.

Her lips were painted with something pink and shiny. I took pleasure knowing I'd be kissing that off soon.

"Hi there!" she said, giving me a chaste kiss as she entered my apartment.

She spun around for a three-sixty degree view, looking all kinds of pleased.

"Wow. Look at this!" she said, gazing down on Central Park.

I pulled the cork out of some nice red sangiovese and poured us both a glass.

"And this is an awesome kitchen," she added.

"Thank you and cheers," I said. I couldn't take my eyes off her.

Her gaze locked with mine, and she tilted her head, giving me the smile that I'd found captivating from the first time I'd met her. All thoughts of my earlier, unpleasant conversation with Minette, were forgotten.

She set down her wine glass. "Okay. I have to see the little miss." She clapped her hands and jumped like an excited kid.

I was thrilled when someone wanted to see my little girl. I was turning into such a sap, but all my friends told me daughters did that to you.

"C'mon. She's sleeping."

I took Avril by the hand and led her into Ruby's bedroom. With the nightlight on, the room was just bright enough to see my little angel, who was once again sleeping with her head turned to the side and her arms spread out over her head. Her tiny double chin and stubby nose swelled my heart with pride.

What could I say? I just couldn't help it.

"She is absolutely delicious," Avril whispered, stroking a finger down Ruby's pudgy cheek. The baby stirred, and Avril snatched her hand back.

"Don't worry," I whispered. "Pretty much nothing can wake her once she's down for the night."

"Does she sleep all the way through?"

I took her hand to lead her from the room. I had other things on my mind, things that could not take place in a baby's room.

"She sleeps through the night now. In fact, she will straight through 'til when the nanny arrives in the morning. I've been lucky that way."

I closed Ruby's door lightly behind us, and Avril and I settled into the living room sofa with our wine after making sure the baby monitor was close by.

"Do you mind if I ask about Ruby's mom?"

She could ask or do anything she wanted to me. I would never be able to say no to this woman. "Her mom is not in the picture. She left right after the baby was born. Told me I was on my own, and said goodbye."

"Oh my god, Chase. That's incredible."

The compassion in her eyes just about killed me.

I swirled wine around my glass. "It was hard. It still

is hard. But you know how they say the worst thing that happens to you can also be the best?" Goddamn if I didn't feel a lump in my throat. I took a swig of my wine to swallow it away.

Avril nodded slowly.

"It was all for the best. I don't want Ruby to have a reluctant or uncommitted mother. That would hurt her more than the day when she's old enough to realize her mother didn't want her."

Avril squeezed my hand. "I'm sorry."

"Thank you." The sincerity in her words that was such a contrast to the bullshit Minette had just tried to lay on me. It was uncanny.

Warmth worked its way through me, easing the tension that telling the story of Ruby's mother had brought up. I popped up to get us more wine, when the door buzzed again. I pressed the intercom buzzer.

"Hello?"

"Hey, buddy. I'm downstairs."

"Come on up." I buzzed my building's front door open.

"Was that *Sumner?*"

"Yep," I said, returning to the sofa.

"Oh, cool. But why is he coming over?" she asked, beyond puzzled.

"Well, he wasn't doing anything tonight, and we thought we'd surprise you."

The question mark clouding her face was replaced

by a sexy look that told me we might be on the same page.

"You're so fucking beautiful," I murmured, and I leaned toward her.

Placing a hand behind her head, I pulled her in to meet my kiss. She smelled of light perfume and expensive red wine, and her lips were sexy and pliable beneath mine.

Shit, I didn't want to stop, but I heard Sumner approaching. Not that I had to stop for *him*, but someone had to open the damn door.

"More of this later, baby," I said, kissing her on the forehead.

"Hey, Sum. C'mon in," I said, welcoming my friend.

'Thanks, dude," Sumner said, his tall frame just fitting under the doorjamb.

He spied Avril on the sofa and made a beeline for her.

"Hey, gorgeous. Long time, no see." In the process of giving her a bear hug he picked her up off the floor like she was nothing more than a ragdoll.

"Well, well," she said, her eyes twinkling. She looked from one of us to the other. "What am I gonna do with you two?"

Sumner and I looked at each other.

We had a few ideas.

21

AVRIL

Oh my.

Sumner had joined Chase and me. What was that all about?

He'd greeted me with a hug, and the scent of him brought back the flood of emotions that had struck me the evening before when he'd shared the story about his dad with me.

And of course made me come. Multiple times.

And now that I was looking at Chase, my heart swelled at how he'd rebuilt his life to take care of a little girl whose mother didn't want her.

God, I loved those guys. And Ash and Gio. Shit. Did I just say *love*? We were bonding over pain and healing with shared passion. What could be better than that?

"Sum, you want a glass?" Chase asked, waving the bottle for him to see.

"Yessir. I'm exhausted from last night…" He looked directly at me. "But I could have a little wine before I pass out for the night."

All right. I was beginning to see how this worked. The guys didn't mind, and in fact seemed to like it, when I'd been with another of the group. And if they were okay with it, I sure as hell wasn't going to be ashamed or embarrassed. I walked over to the kitchen where Chase was pouring.

"Look at these marble countertops. They're amazing," I said.

Sumner smoothed his hand over the white surface shot through with grey streaks. "I know I loved it when I lived here," he said.

"What? You lived here?" I asked.

They both nodded.

"Yeah. Back when we were starting up the biz, we were roommates," Sumner said.

"Yup. Just like in college," Chase added.

Wow. Quite the bond.

And they were quite the pair—Sumner, tall with dark hair, and at least on that day, utterly sexy facial scruff, and Chase, blond with an adorable baby face. Maybe I'd start calling them "salt and pepper."

They were so damn handsome.

And kind.

And smart.

And sexy…

Focus, girl.

"Is that when you developed your special… um, appetites?" I asked.

The guys looked at each other.

"It was, in fact," Sumner said.

Chase approached me and hooked a finger under my chin, tilting my face towards his.

Without turning away, he asked, "Sum. What do you think we should do with our pretty lady, here?"

"I've got some ideas."

Damn if the strongest shivers didn't just run down my spine. I reached for the kitchen counter to steady myself.

"I'll bet," Chase said, lowering his mouth to mine.

My eyes fell closed as strong hands brushed my shoulders and stroked the length of my arms. They worked their way to my waist, where they could almost encircle me with their long, thick fingers. A growing erection pushed against my backside, not to mention Chase's, which was pressed against my front.

"I think we should return to the living room," he said, leading me by the hand.

I grabbed my wine glass and followed. I could still feel his kiss on my lips, and every inch of me vibrated with anticipation.

"Sum, why don't you sit there," Chase said, pointing.

My tall friend settled into an expensive leather

chair, leaning back and smiling with his wine in one hand, his long legs stretched before him.

Chase grabbed the chair opposite.

Hmm. I was left standing in the middle. With both men looking me up and down, it was both oddly uncomfortable and also a turn-on. I could only imagine they were thinking about how to have their ways with me. And other naughty things.

During a different time in my life—hell, just a couple weeks ago—I would have been crawling out of my skin with embarrassment. But now I felt powerful. And beautiful. And in control of my life. Well, almost

So I decided to take charge. No time like the present, and all that…

I kicked my flats off and put my hands on the side zip of my capri pants. But I was going to make this last, and I turned around slowly so I could see each guy, and so they could each get a good look at me. My nipples were hard and pointed, and I could feel the throbbing inside my pants. While I might have been ready to go, I was in no hurry.

Take your time.

Which made me wonder why Sumner had joined us when I'd been with him just the night before. Didn't he want Chase to have his quality time with me? Unless… they each wanted to see me with the other guy…

I guess that was the sharing thing in a nutshell.

And shit, I'd never been with two guys.

While swaying to the background music, I slowly

unzipped my pants, let them drop, and kicked them aside. When I untied the bow on my halter, I was left standing in nothing more than a very skimpy, sheer thong that scarcely concealed my bare pussy.

One of the guys—I wasn't sure which—quietly whistled his approval. Since they were the ones I wanted to impress, I took that as a compliment.

Since Sumner had had me the night before, I padded over to Chase and straddled him in his seat. His hands immediately flew to my breasts, pulling my girls together and sucking one aching nipple, then moving to the other.

While he did this, I ground lightly on the erection straining inside his jeans. This sent a spark right into my throbbing core that echoed through my belly, leaving my flesh on fire. Then his lips found mine for a lush kiss.

Sumner had come up behind me and pulled off the ponytail holder I'd placed on the end of my braid. He fumbled with my plaited hair, and in moments had it free. As my hair tumbled down my back, he took fist-fuls of it and inhaled deeply, sighing.

With Chase's hands on the sides of my face as he kissed me, my breasts were now free for Sumner's wandering hands. He reached around me, pulling on my aching nipples until I squirmed. But sandwiched between the two of them, with nowhere to go.

Which I guess was kind of the point.

And I loved it.

Sumner kept a hand on one of my breasts while his other wandered into my panties. His thick fingers dove between my soaked lips. Once he found my opening, he plunged the tips of two fingers inside me. I pulled back from Chase's kiss to scream with the pleasure of being entered.

And it was only the beginning.

"Take her panties off, Sum," Chase growled.

Sumner lifted me off Chase's lap to a wobbly standing position. He slipped my panties to my ankles, and helped me step out of them.

"C'mon, baby," Chase said, gesturing for me to return to his lap. "I want to feel that shaved pussy of yours."

Oh my.

The raw, dirty talk was new to me, but it was so hot it nearly pushed me over my edge. It just seethed power and confidence and I felt so safe, being with men who knew what they wanted and weren't afraid to say it. And I loved that what they wanted was *me*.

Sumner's thumb traveled to my clit, where he made big circles, sending sparks of lightening shooting from my core to every extremity.

I pulled Chase's polo over his head to reveal his muscled chest, then fumbled with his belt buckle and fly.

Behind me, I heard the rustling of Sumner throwing his own clothes aside, which was confirmed when he reached for my tits and pressed his ferociously hard cock against my naked back.

Chase lifted his ass, and me with him, just enough to get his pants to his ankles. Before kicking them aside, he reached into one of his pockets, producing a condom.

"Sum, she's hot, isn't she?" he said.

"Fuck yeah, buddy. And I love these tits," he said, playing with aching nipples.

A morsel of shame shot through me, that two men were talking about me like I was a toy—a *fuck toy*—but I took a deep breath and pushed it away. Theirs was a different way to play, and they'd invited me to join. I didn't have to do anything I didn't want to, and that was abundantly clear.

And I wanted these guys. Badly.

In a moment, Chase was rolling the condom over his long cock. When he was finished, he put his hands on my waist, maneuvering me to hover right above him.

"I'll let you drive, baby," he said, not looking away from me for a sec.

Well, then.

I arched my back to throw my breasts in his face and lowered myself over his erection. It bounced over my screaming clit and slipped down between my soaked lips, swollen with need and begging for relief.

I was breathlessly turned on by the four hands roving my body.

Lowering myself onto Chase's cock head, I gyrated my hips for a little tease. A sly smile spread across his face. He knew exactly what I was doing. And he liked it.

So I slammed down his entire length, the girth of him taking my breath away. I held still for a moment to adjust, and then began to rock my hips back and forth, grinding deeper into him.

"Fuck, Avril. You are fucking hot, baby," he growled. "Slow down, or I'll come too fast."

His grip on my waist grew tighter as he grew closer to losing any control he'd had. Gritting his teeth, he threw his head back while I held onto the sofa behind him. Sumner had moved to my left side and presented me with his cock. Right at the level of my mouth.

I was really going to have two guys. At once. Like, at the same time.

Me.

I grabbed Sumner at his root and directed him deep inside my mouth where I sucked 'til my cheeks hollowed and I could scarcely breathe. Blood roared through my ears, and I think I heard myself somehow screaming with a mouthful of cock, but I couldn't be absolutely sure.

Chase moaned, then growled, and his cock grew harder inside me—as if that were possible. He exploded in an endless orgasm, which sparked another for me, causing me to suck Sumner with such vigor that he spurted in my mouth, his cum running down my chin.

The three of us rolled through our ferocious orgasms together.

LATER, I lay on Chase's bed between the two guys, their magnificent nakedness shiny with perspiration in the light thrown by the bedside lamp.

Their breathing had slowed, as had my heartbeat, and the room smelled slightly like my perfume, and a lot like the sex of people healing from wounds that might someday close.

22

GIO

I'D JUST ARRIVED AT OUR SECOND KINK LAB PARTY AT Avril's gallery, stepping into the transformed space filled with New York's elite—well, at least the kinky elite.

It was a show of the rich, powerful, and beautiful. Even the air felt expensive.

Bellissimo.

I wove through the room, greeting our guests, until I spied Ash across the room. He was trying to extricate himself from one of the many women who pursued him at things like this, women who were drawn by his dark, exotic looks, and his exceptional height.

"Ash," I called, in my attempt to rescue him.

He excused himself from the *bella signora,* feigning great remorse.

It's not that he wouldn't have liked any of these ladies under other circumstances, but when he was hosting, he tried to keep his clothes on.

Sometimes it worked. Sometimes it didn't.

But we were all interested in only one woman these days. Unfortunately, that obliterated the chances of any of the other ladies at the party spending time with us.

"Guys!" a voice boomed.

"Shit. Who invited him?" Ash muttered.

"I think it was Sum. He felt badly for him," I answered.

Smith rushed across the room to us, his eyes nearly bugging out of his head at the scene around him.

On one hand, I couldn't blame the man. Everyone was like that the first time. But most people had enough game to try to hide it a little.

But not Smith. *Cretino.*

"We need to keep an eye on this one tonight," I said, lowering my voice as Smith neared.

"Agreed."

"Damn, guys. This is some serious *shit*," Smith said, taking a too-big swig of his scotch in one hand and adjusting his trousers with the other.

I really wasn't sure why Sumner had included Smith in this part of our lives. The guy had the maturity of a *ragazzo* going through puberty. If he misbehaved by bothering anyone, and we had to kick him out, things would be awfully awkward at work the next day.

And the chances of his misbehaving were *very* high. *Merda.*

"Good to see you, Smith," I said.

"Thanks for inviting me, dude," he said, slapping me on the back.

I *hadn't* invited him, but I wasn't going to point that out.

I decided to address the elephant in the room. I knew the other guys would eventually do so, too, and I thought the more of us he heard it from, the better.

"Smith." I put an arm around him and walked him to a quiet corner. "*Amico,* I must ask that you behave tonight."

He pulled away from me, outrage splashed all over his face.

"What the hell does that mean, Gio? *Behave?*"

I inhaled deeply. "Smith, I did not mean to insult you. But we have rules for the club. You have to take it slow, and be careful to not drink too much."

"Don't worry, Gio. I'll be *fine.*"

And with that, he stormed off to god knew where. All I could do was hope he didn't piss off any of our guests.

And hope he wasn't invited next time.

IT WAS another hour before I found the beautiful Avril, shining in a slim white silk dress with her masses of black hair twisted into some confection at the nape of her neck. A neck I was dying to lay my lips on.

"There you are, *mia cara.*"

I pulled her toward me, taking a deep inhale where her neck met her shoulder. The best spot on a woman, if you asked me.

"Gio!" she purred, taking my hands and laying a sweet kiss on my lips.

"Shall we walk?" I asked.

Hooking her hand through my elbow, she fell in with me.

"You know, I am still blown away by these parties. I wonder if the novelty ever wears off?" she asked, looking around discreetly.

"No, I don't think it ever does. Or if it does—if it becomes mundane—well, I imagine then you stop coming."

I led her to a small room we'd created with the help of some floating white curtains. The space held a couple love seats, already occupied, facing a large tufted cushion where a man and two women were playing.

"Let's watch for a moment, *cara,*" I said.

I doubted she'd ever been with a woman, but you never know with American girls. Word was, they all tried their hands at sapphic love in college.

We stood at the entrance to the room, lit just enough to cast the most beautiful glow on anyone close by, especially the two undressed women in the middle. One was thin as a rail, with short, close-cropped hair, like a little sprite. The other, a curvy woman with wild black hair reminded me of the girls from *Napoli* I'd see on summer vacations when I was a kid. They were both vaguely familiar from my time spent on the city's charity circuit.

With them was a guy I also knew—preppy as a Ralph Lauren model and with tastes that raised even my eyebrows.

He was what my friends called an *ass man*.

"What do you think, darling?"

Avril was mesmerized. She didn't have to say a thing. It was written all over her face.

The two women alternately kissed each other, then the guy, and then each other again. The man lay the dark-haired woman on her back and gently spread her legs as far apart as they would go. He spoke quietly to the blonde as he guided her between the other woman's legs. He ran his hand up and down the lips of the brunette's sex, and then pointed for the blonde to do the same.

As instructed, she began to stroke the woman's pussy, leaving the brunette gasping and writhing on the mattress under her. Then, the guy placed his hand on the back of the blonde's head and guided her face directly into the woman's sex. Without hesitation, the blonde eagerly lapped at the pussy before her, with a great focus on the woman's clit.

I glanced over at Avril, whose mouth was slightly parted. She caught me looking.

"Um...wow. That's really something," she whispered.

In the meantime, the guy had positioned himself behind the blonde. He looked down at her ass with admiration written all over his face, and he spread her cheeks by taking fistfuls of her tiny behind. She squirmed and pushed against him, clearly relishing the sensation.

He lowered his face to her ass and extended his tongue to her most private parts. She moaned with her mouth full of the other woman's pussy and began pushing back into the guy's face.

And with his free hand, he stroked himself to beat the band.

Mamma mia.

And of course, I had a hard-on that wouldn't quit.

Avril turned to me, gripping my hand tightly.

"Can we go somewhere? I'm feeling a little light-headed."

"Come with me." I led her to a quiet corner where we found a seat on an empty bench. I spotted Ash on the other side of the room and waved him over.

"Ash, would you get Avril a cool glass of water, please?" I asked.

"Sure. You okay, angel?" he asked.

She looked up, a little pale with a light sheen of sweat on her forehead.

"I'm good. I think the champagne went to my head or something. And standing there, watching those people play..." She closed her eyes and took a deep breath.

Ash returned with the water and took a seat on the other site of our girl.

"Ahhh," she said, finishing it. "That was exactly what I needed. Much better."

"That's good, Avril, because I am really wanting to kiss you," Ash said.

He looked at me, and I just smiled and nodded *yes*.

She leaned toward him, and he took her face in his hands. Initially, he just brushed her lips with his, but then he applied more pressure. She moaned lightly, caught in Ash's hunger.

He pulled back from her.

"Now you kiss Gio, baby," he said.

She smiled and turned to me. The moment I'd been waiting for all night.

Our lips met, and just like during the first time we'd kissed, some sort of lightening struck through me, where I knew I was in the right place, with the right woman.

It was the damnedest thing. I'd heard of that happening before, but not to me.

As I kissed her, Ash pulled the zipper down the

back of her dress and pushed the garment forward so it fell to her waist.

Her delicious breasts were bare, and my hands went right to them. Ash, in the meantime, kissed the back of her neck until she whimpered in my mouth.

"I'm going to slide my fingers under your dress, Angel," Ash murmured, pushing the white silk aside to get to our girl's sweet pussy.

Suddenly Blu appeared right before us. "I've been looking for you guys all over!"

Avril's eyes popped open.

"Av, get your dress back on. You guys," he said, looking at Ash and me, "c'mon."

He pulled Avril's dress back up and zipped it closed before she could even register what was going on. Ash and I stood there wondering how we'd been cock-blocked by a gay man with red hair and a gap in his teeth. And a bow tie.

I put my hand on Blu's arm. "What's going on? Are you okay?"

He waved frantically for us to get up and follow him. "Yeah, I'm okay. I mean, I'm not okay. *C'mon*," he urged, starting to walk away.

Avril finally got her voice back. "Blu, what the hell is going on?" she asked.

His voice cracked. "There's been an accident."

23

AVRIL

BLU YANKED ME BY THE HAND AND HALF-RAN, HALF-walked me past the two women and one man I'd been watching, across the gallery, up the stairs to my office.

"Blu, what the hell is going on?" I asked repeatedly.

But he wouldn't answer.

I looked over my shoulder to find Gio and Ash right behind us with their long strides.

It wasn't out of character for Blu to get upset—even hysterical—but it *was* unlike him to hold off on telling me exactly what was going on.

Why was he waiting? What the hell was happening?

When the four of us got to my office, having rushed through the party like there was a fire somewhere, and turning more than a few heads at our haste, Sumner and Chase were already there.

Something about them was different.

Sumner had a cup of water in his hand instead of his usual scotch on the rocks. His eyes looked tired. Chase was tapping the corner of my desk, which he was half-sitting on, like it was a drum set. Completely lost in thought.

Maybe the parties were too much for them with the demands of RESLR.

I turned to see Blu blow his nose.

"Okay. Now what the hell is going on?" Ash demanded.

Sumner took a deep breath. "Smith left the party awhile ago, although none of us saw him leave. Apparently, he'd had too much to drink. He crashed his car on the West Side Highway."

"No…" Gio murmured.

"Oh my god," I murmured.

Chase shook his head. "It…it was fatal."

I felt like someone slugged me in the stomach, and I sank into my desk chair. The horror of losing my Lisette rushed over me like it had happened only yesterday.

"He's gone," Blu added.

I hadn't really known Smith, but I knew the guys had been close with him since their college years, and in the last couple, they'd taken him on at the firm. He'd seemed nice enough to me, if a bit frat-boyish.

Sumner walked toward the door. "I have to get to the hospital."

I finally found my voice. "How did you find out?"

"I was listed as his emergency contact. I guess he listed me last year after his parents passed away."

He stepped toward me and gave me a kiss on the cheek. "I'll call you guys later. Sorry to leave you with closing up the party," he said.

"Don't worry, *amico*. We'll take care of everything." Gio gave him a big hug and patted him on the back on his way out.

Chase stopped his tapping. "I'm sorry to do this to you all, but I gotta get home to my Ruby. I can't be away from her for another moment."

"It's okay, Chase. We'll take care of everything," Blu said.

I approached him and put my hands on his face. "Kiss the baby for me, will you?" And I gave him a tender kiss of his own.

Ash took charge. "All right. We need to wrap the party up. It's nearly eleven p.m., so no one will suspect anything. Blu, will you have the cleaning and moving crews here in one hour?"

He turned to Gio. "Go tell the bartenders to close down. If anybody asks, tell them to say they ran out of ice."

Gio and Blu nodded and left.

"What about us?" I asked.

"I'll walk around and tell a few folks it's closing time. The others will soon follow."

"And me?"

"Can you take the door? Maybe get that beautiful smile back on your face?" he asked.

"Of course." I headed downstairs.

While I said goodbye to the folks who were already heading out, I couldn't help but think of the car accident that changed my life and took my sister from me. The guilt and shame that flooded over me was nearly as strong as the day it happened, and it was all I could do to keep from losing my shit in front of the guests I was bidding a good night to.

And like Lisette's accident, I felt partially responsible for Smith's.

Yeah, I knew he was basically the office clown, and that the guys had questionable respect for him, but he had to be only in his thirties. And he'd been at a party at *my* gallery and had left for the evening without saying goodbye to anyone.

A lump lodged in my throat as I smiled brightly at the departing guests, squeezing their hands and patting their arms. My voice no longer worked.

WHEN THE LAST guest had gone, I wandered around the gallery, now being quickly transformed from a night as a sex club back to its normal state. It had been a good evening by most measures, with our usual full house.

Some of the artwork had even sold, which Blu had taken care of.

"Hey," I said weakly when I found Blu, his eyes red and bloodshot.

"I can't fucking believe this," he said. "I mean, we all went to college together."

"I'm sorry Blu. I'm sorry you lost a friend. Sorry all you guys lost a friend."

My shoulders trembled and then began to heave. I buried my face in Blu's chest, and my quiet tears fell. I knew he'd joined me when I heard him sniffling.

I lifted my head.

"Blu, I can't have any more parties here in the gallery."

"Well, I can understand that. But sweetie, Smith's accident had nothing to do with you, or the gallery. It could have happened on his way home from anything."

"I don't know, Blu. It just wouldn't feel right. I never should have had parties here to begin with. This is an art gallery, not a night club."

"Okay. I get it. I respect your decision, and I know the guys will, too."

I gave him a kiss on the cheek. "Thanks."

"For what?" he asked.

I shrugged. Where to begin? The list was long. "For…just being you. And being there for me."

He held my hand. "'Course, baby. You're my bestie."

"And thank you for introducing me to the guys."

A wicked look crossed his face. "You sure seem to like them."

Frowning, I nodded. "Yeah, of course. What's not to like?"

Blu nodded. "I know. I've been friends with them for years, and I wouldn't have let a single one of them near you if they weren't the high-quality men I know you deserve. Unlike that douche-y ex of yours."

"Soon-to-be-ex. Actually, not soon enough."

"What are you going to do about the guys?"

I looked around to make sure no one was within earshot.

"I'm not sure. Sumner is so smart and serious, and he looks out for everyone. Chase is just a pile of mush. He's so in love with his baby. Gio is about the most charming man I've ever met, with his European style and manners. And Ash is my wild, exotic animal—a bit unpredictable. And they're all so goddamn sexy."

"Sounds like you hit the guy lottery, my friend. Or should I say the *harem* lottery?" He laughed.

My stomach knotted, just as it had every time I tried to figure out how to handle my predicament. "Well, I won something, that's for sure. I'm just don't know what yet. I mean, at some point, I have to choose one of them. *If* they even want me. I don't know how I'll do that when the time comes."

"You'll figure it out, sweetie. And I'll be there right by your side." He glanced at his watch. "But tonight, I am leaving you in the capable hands of Ash and Gio, if that's okay."

Ah. It was Blu's turn to have fun, away from the heterosexual world he'd been immersed in all night.

"Yeah. Go. Do you have one of your hook ups?" I asked.

He stood and pulled me to my feet. "You know it. Actually, this guy I've seen a couple times now. How 'bout the three of us have brunch, some time?"

Whoa. He'd actually seen someone more than one time, *and* he wanted me to meet him?

"Well, well, well. My little Blu is finally growing up…"

"Oh, shut up, you little whore. At least I'm not fucking four men." He leaned toward my ear as he saw Ash approaching. "And I'm so jealous of you, you little beotch."

I waved him off. "You love me. I know you do."

He gave me a quick peck on the lips and took off for the door.

"What a night," I said to Ash.

I suddenly felt like I'd been hit by a truck. I could only imagine how the guys felt.

"Let's go home," he said. "Gio!" he called.

"Right here, *fratello*. Ready to go?" Gio asked.

"Yeah. Our car is out front. The crew will finish everything else up."

We headed for the door of my gallery, my refuge in

the storm that had become my life. I walked between both of my guys, holding their hands in each of mine.

We hopped into the back of Ash's car.

"Where to, Mr. Ash?" the driver asked over his shoulder.

But I spoke up first. "My place."

Ash and Gio nodded, and we headed home.

24

ASH

After I'd given the driver Avril's address, I must have conked out.

Next thing I knew, we were stopped in front of her building, and she was shaking me awake.

I looked around, initially unsure of where I was. But when I realized my beautiful Avril was hovering over me, trying to get me inside and to bed, a quiet calm washed over me.

I could get used to waking up to that angelic face on a regular basis.

The three of us stumbled into Avril's elevator, silent and numb from the news of Smith's death.

He'd been at college with Blu and the rest of us. He'd always been somewhat of an ass, but we let him tag along with us.

After graduation, he'd moved to LA for several years to try his hand working for the big studios as a finance guy. But sometimes you just can't shake the East Coast out of someone.

He eventually found his way back to New York, and we made him a limited partner. He got his name on our masthead, but since he wasn't one of the founders, he didn't have as much influence over our business as the rest of us.

I think he was just happy to be home. Never once did he mention missing the sunshine, palm trees, and swimming pools. That always kind of surprised me. I guess that made him a true New Yorker.

And now he was gone. Just like that. We'd invited him to his first Kink Lab—not without some trepidation—but we wanted to give him a chance and see if he could hang. Gio had a little 'talk' with him. It undoubtedly pissed him off, but he had to be warned.

A lot of good it did.

I had no idea what happened for him that night. I'd not seen him since he first arrived, but I did know he drank too much and got behind the wheel of his car.

It just made no sense. He could have taken a cab or gotten someone's driver to give him a lift home. God knew enough of the people at the party had arrived in limos. But for some insane reason, he drove.

I shot Sumner a text to see if he was still at the hospital. I wasn't sure what they did when someone died, but I knew Sum had to identify him and probably sign papers since Smith's parents were gone and he was an only child.

Sum?

Hey

You good? Things ok?

Yeah. It's all so goddam unnecessary. This didn't have to happen

I know, brother. Thanks for taking care of our friend

And even though right then was not the time to think about it, I couldn't help but wonder what impact his death would have on RESLR, or Kink Lab.

We entered Avril's sprawling apartment. She kicked off her shoes, and Ash and I tossed our coats over chairs and loosened our ties.

"Anyone care for a drink?" she asked.

"That would be *buonissimo, cara,*" Gio said.

Christ, even at this late hour, when we were all exhausted and stunned by Smith's death, Gio managed to sound elegant and in control. He'd always been that way. Made him a star with the ladies.

We sat, sipping our cognac, while Avril excused herself. From where I sat in the living room, I could see her bed, and it was seriously calling to me. I had to fight the urge to kick off my shoes and get under the covers for the night.

But I wasn't going to do that. I wanted a bit more time with my lovely Avril.

And wouldn't you know it, she came back into the living room wearing a lush silk robe, sort of pearl-colored like her dress of earlier in the evening. Only this time, she wasn't wearing anything underneath. And the silk was sheer, as light-colored fabrics often are.

Her brown nipples stabbed at the thin fabric covering them, rousing my dick to attention. If I thought I might be too tired to get it up, well, Avril had proved me wrong just by walking into the room.

I watched as she crossed to get her drink, the robe fabric draping over her ass and showing off her bum's slight jiggle. I glanced over at Gio. He was in about the same shape I was—mesmerized.

The evening was late, and I had no time to waste. I got up and took Avril's drink from her. I was almost too tired to make a pass at our girl. Almost, but not quite.

I pulled the bow that held her robe closed. The silk fluttered open, revealing the inner swell of her breasts, her smooth, soft stomach, and a completely shaved pussy.

Goddamn. It was all I could do to remain upright.

I glanced back to see Gio watching, wearing the slightest smile on his face. I pushed Avril's robe back over her shoulders. It puddled at her feet as it fell, leaving her standing before us, gloriously naked, and sexy as fuck.

I led her to the bedroom and to the edge of her bed,

where she lay back, running her hands over herself. I unbuttoned my starched shirt, my gaze locked with hers, and tossed it aside. I didn't bother with the rest of my clothes. I was too eager to kneel before her and pull her legs up over my shoulders.

Before I dove into her delicious pussy, I saw Gio at the side of the bed, removing his own clothes.

And what a delicious pussy it was. I gently pried apart her swollen lips and dragged my tongue along her slit from top to bottom. I lingered for a moment at her juicy opening, and then moved up to her hard clit.

I circled her sensitive bud and zeroed in on it with a soft suction. She moaned breathily, and I looked up to see Gio next to her on the bed, his cock in her tight grip.

Fuck, yeah. I loved sharing a beautiful woman with my buddy.

Avril began to writhe as I filled her pussy with two, then three fingers and pumped, stretching her while I continued to work her clit. Within moments, she was thrashing on the bed above me, bucking her hips, and pulling Gio's cock toward her mouth.

That's my girl.

With her mouth full, she exploded in a quiet rage, her tight little body wracked with spasms. Gio pulled out just in time to come all over her tits.

I stood to shed the rest of my clothes, but before I did, I grabbed a condom out of my pocket. As I sheathed myself, my gaze remained glued to Avril. She was so fucking gorgeous with her black hair fanning over the bed and down across her breasts. I'd never be able to take my eyes off her.

Gio scooted her up on the bed, and I flipped her over onto her stomach. Positioning myself behind her, I leaned close to her ear.

"Are you good, baby? Are you ready for me?"

She nodded so hard, her hair flew in every direction.

"Fuck me, Ash. Please," she begged.

I pressed my cock at her searing opening, my hands gripping her ass and opening her, so I could see myself fucking her.

She pushed back on me when she was ready, so I slowly gave her all of myself until I was balls-deep inside her.

"God, Ash. Oh…oh…"

Gio reached under her to make small circles on her clit. The extra stimulation drove her wild. She bucked back into me until my balls pulled in tight, and I couldn't see or hear. All I could do was feel with my cock.

And I felt goddamn good.

I exploded inside her, my hips propelling me further into her with every violent spurt. She was breathing so hard, I thought she might hyperventilate.

When I'd pulled out and tossed the condom, Gio and I pulled her down on the bed with us, wrapping her in all our limbs with both satisfaction and the sadness of knowing nothing in life was certain, and that you could lose it all in a moment.

Like Smith had.

"Guys?" Avril spoke so quietly, I nearly missed what she was saying. "I'm selling the gallery."

25

AVRIL

THE SUN SPLASHED ME IN THE FACE THE NEXT MORNING, rudely nudging me out of a deep sleep.

Ash and Gio were on either side of me, beginning to stir, too. But before they were fully awake, I had the chance to admire them. The sun reflected off a light sheen of perspiration on Ash's dark brown skin, and Gio's normally perfect faux-hawk had been destroyed by bed head. The two of them were perfect.

Just like Sumner and Chase.

Christ, what was I doing messing around with four guys? And having sex club parties in my gallery? And buying dresses cut down to my navel at Barneys?

Was I out of my mind?

Just then, Gio rolled over, swinging an arm around my waist. At nearly the same time, Ash's hand moved under the sheets and when it collided with mine, grasped two of my fingers.

No, I wasn't out of my mind. Not at all. I'd never felt safer, or more cherished, in my life.

I could have laid there forever.

Someone's phone buzzed, and the guys gradually woke up. I wasn't sure whose it was, but I wasn't about to move as long as I was encased by two beautiful men.

"Hey. Good morning," Ash said, releasing my hand and sitting up.

He crawled out of the bed, stretching and yawning, and shit, did he look delicious naked. He unselfconsciously scratched at his balls while looking around the room for the buzzing phone.

"Gio, it's your phone. Here, bro," he said, tossing it in his direction.

Gio raised one hand above the sheets just in time to catch it.

"It's Sumner," he said, swiping open.

"*Buongiorno,* Sumner. I'm guessing it was a late night for you?"

I let Gio continue his conversation and popped out of bed to make coffee for the three of us. Ash pulled on his trousers and followed me to the kitchen.

"What's this about selling the gallery?" Ash asked, with his eyebrows raised.

I should have known that was coming. I'd shared my news just as we were falling asleep—I guess to avoid the inevitable conversation.

And now I felt like a little kid about to get into trouble. I busied myself with the coffee to avoid looking at him. "I guess after last night, losing Smith and all, it just seems like a bad omen. Something just doesn't feel right. Like the place is tainted."

Ash settled into one of the stools at the kitchen counter and accepted a mug of steaming coffee. "Avril, it's tragic what happened to Smith, but it has nothing to do with your gallery, or Kink Lab for that matter. I mean, I'm sad about it too. I've known him since we were roommates in college."

"I'm sorry, Ash. You know I lost my sister in a car crash." God it still hurt to say those words out loud. It was as if by not speaking about the loss out loud, I could perpetually keep it from being real.

"I did know that, baby. One of the other guys told me." Looking down at his coffee, he shook his head. "I can't imagine what that has been like for you."

That familiar tight feeling in my chest was making itself at home again. I took discreet deep breaths. If I didn't get it under control right then, my entire day would be out of whack.

"Sometimes, I can't imagine what it's like, either. And then I realize I'm living in the middle of it," I said.

He walked around the kitchen island to me and pulled on the belt of my bathrobe. It fell open, inviting his warm hands to my breasts.

"I'm going to kiss you now," he said.

"Then shut up and do it."

Just as his lips met mine, there was a loud throat clearing from the bedroom doorway.

Damn if Gio wasn't standing there in his unclothed glory, the smooth mounds of muscle all over his body catching the sun streaming in my windows. I followed the perfect splay of chest hair to the thin line over his tummy, to his uncircumcised cock, which was at rest but nonetheless gorgeous.

I pulled my robe closed and poured a cup of coffee for him, too. "You'd better put on some clothes, you brute, or the three of us will never get out of the house this morning," I said.

He grabbed me by the waist and kissed me deeply, while Ash rolled his eyes and smiled.

Damn, I was one lucky girl.

"How was your call with Sumner?" I asked.

"About as you would expect. Weary and sad," Gio said, shaking his head. He headed back into the bedroom and started to pull on his clothes.

I plopped down on the edge of the bed to watch.

Ash stood in the doorway.

"*Mia cara,* what is this about selling your gallery? Surely you know that's completely *pazzo.*"

I twisted my robe's tie. "After last night…I don't know. I mean, it's really left a bad taste in my mouth. And not only that, but my ex's name is on the lease, and it looks like that could be an issue. I found out last night right before the party. I didn't want to say anything then."

Ash looked pissed. "What is wrong with that asshole? He can't force you to close."

I was blown away by the guys' support. I hadn't known them for all that long—well, not *intimately* anyway—and they totally had my back. Like we'd been friends forever. Or lovers forever.

"You guys. Thank you. I love your support."

Gio pulled on his jacket, kissed my forehead, and headed for the door. "We know, *cara*, you must make your own decisions. You are a smart, strong woman. It's what we love about you."

Love?

Ash's head snapped in Gio's direction, and they exchanged a look.

What the hell was going on? I looked from one to the other.

"Let's talk later, *bella*. I just got off the phone with Sumner. He was up all night taking care of Smith's affairs. I want to get to the office to see what I can do to help."

"I'll head out with you, Gio," Ash said, looking at his watch. "I want to get in touch with anyone Smith might have had meetings with." His last few words broke up, and he struggled to hold on to his composure.

I ran over to him.

"Oh, baby, I'm sorry." I kissed him, and then Gio.

"Look," he said, "let's all of us get together tonight. We need to talk about some things."

All of us? Like all five of us?

"Sure. Let's do it," I said.

And they were gone.

When I finally looked at the time on my phone, I realized it was still only seven a.m.

I had no appointments at the gallery that day, so I tossed my robe aside and slipped under the covers, pulling my down comforter up to my chin. The bed still smelled like my beautiful men—a mix of something spicy and sexy. It was as if they were still right there in bed with me. I balled myself up into a comfortable little knot and imagined their arms around me, wandering, exploring, and making me feel damn good.

I MUST HAVE DOZED off with a smile on my face because I woke up with one. My phone had buzzed long enough to drag me out of my extra snooze.

Christ, it was nearly ten a.m.

I swiped my phone open. "Hi," I said.

"Jesus, are you still in fucking bed? Get up you lazy bones," Blu shrieked.

I propped myself up on two pillows. "Hi. Yeah, I'm still in bed. I can't believe it. I went back to sleep for a bit after Ash and Gio left—"

"Oh. My. God. You were with them both? You little whore!" He cackled so loudly, I had to pull the phone from my ear.

"Well, yeah. What did you think I was doing, asking them to take numbers and wait in the hall?"

That really got him. He was howling with laughter so hard, he couldn't catch his breath. I could just picture his gap-toothed smile.

And you know what? It *was* funny. I mean, how in the hell did someone date men who wanted to *share*? What was the protocol? Did you rotate nights, like on that cable show, *Big Love*?

Yuck. I never liked that show.

Blu finally caught his breath from laughing. "Okay, ho-bag. Get dressed. Let's have lunch in honor of Smith, and then we'll going back to Barneys. Juan owes me a favor."

Oh god. I could only imagine for what.

AFTER LUNCH, Blu and I floated into our favorite store in the entire world.

We wandered through, looking at all beautiful first floor merchandise—handbags, silk scarves, and a little Stella McCartney capsule collection. I didn't dare buy anything, though. I had money in the bank now, thanks to the Kink Lab parties, but I had to make it last. If Devon had his way, I'd not get a penny of our assets after the divorce.

I had to be ready for anything that might come

my way.

Blu took my hand. "C'mon. I didn't come here to look at Chloe handbags. Let's go upstairs and find Juan. He said he'd hook you and me up the last time I sucked his—"

"STOP. I don't need that much detail."

Blu shrugged. "Suit yourself, sister. You better be glad I do what I do, because you are about to get some fabulous new dresses."

26

SUMNER

I HADN'T STARTED THAT WEEK EXPECTING TO BE MAKING funeral arrangements for one of my oldest friends.

But Smith's parents were gone, and he'd been an only child. As far as I knew, he had no other family. I imagined that's why I was his emergency contact.

The call I'd gotten from the police was one of the strangest ones in my life.

"Hello. Is this Mr. Sumner Larlaith?" a voice asked, when the Kink Lab party was in full swing.

I thought it might be someone calling having to do with my father. Occasionally, the press got ahold of my phone number and called me for a quote. Of course, I hung right up on them after an emphatic 'no comment.'

"Yes, this is he," I answered.

"Mr. Larlaith, this is the New York City Police Department."

So it wasn't a reporter.

Holy shit. Had someone made a complaint about Kink Lab? Or stolen my car?

"Is everything okay? What can I do for you?" I asked, my heart rate picking up. I was surprised by the hum of office sounds on the other end of the line, but then I guessed the police department was a twenty-four-seven operation.

"Mr. Larlaith, you are listed as the emergency contact for Mr. Smith Edwards. Do you know him?"

"Yes, of course. He's one of my business partners."

I looked around the club. I could swear I'd seen him just a minute ago. Or had it been an hour ago? Anyway, I was sure he was in the gallery somewhere, hopefully making new friends.

"I'm sorry to tell you, Mr. Larlaith, that Mr. Edwards has been in an accident."

I started pushing through the crowd, searching for Smith. Where the hell was he?

"I think there must be a mistake, officer. He's here with me, at a party in Soho."

"He's been in a car accident on the West Side Highway, sir. He was rushed to the hospital, where they did everything they could. I'm sorry to tell you, he didn't make it."

Was that supposed to be a joke? "Officer, he's here with me."

"Mr. Larlaith, he may have been with you earlier in the evening where he became intoxicated, but he unfortunately got behind the wheel of his car."

I continued pushing through the crowd and climbed the stairs to the loft, where I could get a bird's eye view of the party. Could he actually have left? And *when* would he have left?

"Are you there, sir?" the officer asked.

I didn't see Smith anywhere. My stomach churned and I sank into a chair in a dark corner, forcing a couple deep breaths to see if that might help my shaking hands.

"Yes. Yes, I'm sorry I'm here. I was just running around the party to see if I could find him. But he's not here, like you said."

"Mr. Larlaith, we're going to need you to come to the hospital to identify him and make arrangements for his remains."

What. The. Actual. Fuck.

And that was where the odyssey of putting Smith to rest began. And even though I was exhausted from having been up all night and then going directly to work, I was in an Uber on my way to pick up Gio and then on to Avril's. She'd invited us over for dinner—all four of us guys—because she wanted to talk to us about some things.

Things, she'd said.

Since she left it kind of vague, I asked Gio when he'd hopped into the car, if he knew anything. I knew he and Ash had taken her home the night before. And probably spent the night.

Which I thought was hot as hell. But I couldn't focus on that now, as much as I would have liked to.

"Gio, how'd things go last night? Our girl okay? I'm dying to know what she wants to *talk* about," I said.

"Well, *amico*, she was making noises about selling the gallery, if you can believe it. But Ash and I tried to talk her out of it. Not sure we've convinced her yet. Looks like she told Blu the same thing. He called, thinking I didn't already know."

The streetlights flashed over Gio's face as we drove across the city. Bright, then dark, then bright again.

"Well, it's her choice," I said. "But I don't want her to be hasty about any decisions."

"*Si.* We can always find another place for Kink Lab. I just hate to see her walk away from her passion. She loves art."

We arrived at Avril's, and the doorman let us in.

I had to wonder for a moment what he thought of the men who'd been visiting her recently. New York doormen were a famously discreet group. They *saw* a lot and *said* very little.

Exactly how it should be, and why they received huge Christmas bonuses.

"Hey, have you heard the latest about Avril's ex, Devon Crane?" Gio asked once we were in the privacy of the elevator on our way to her penthouse.

Discreet doormen aside, there were just some things you said only in a very private space.

"Yeah. The bastard's going down. Can't say I'm sorry," I said.

"Well, the man's innocent until proven guilty, but yesterday's indictment does not bode well."

Our conversation screeched to a halt when we saw Avril waiting for us in her doorway. And to be honest, all thoughts about her dickhead ex, and even those about our poor friend Smith, were washed away.

Her hair was bunched into something I didn't know the name for, at the back of her neck. The effect reminded me of a painting of a Flamenco dancer I'd seen last time I'd visited the Met.

But what really got me was the dress.

It was a pale beige, most likely silk, so close to the color of her skin that from a distance, she looked nude. But close up, it was breathtaking. The dress bared one shoulder, was fitted over her breasts, and cinched at the waist with a wide belt. It hit just above her knee, and her sky-high heels made her legs look a mile long. She wore a deep red lipstick that somehow remained just as red after she kissed both Gio and me.

When she turned to walk us into the apartment, I watched her ass jiggle just the tiniest amount under the fabric hugging her hips.

Apparently, our girl was going commando.

"Hey, guys," I said to Chase and Ash, who were

already camped out on her sofa with drinks in their hands.

Avril had scurried off to the kitchen to check on dinner.

I was thinking of helping her…or something like that.

"This place is the shit, isn't it, Sumner?" Ash said, admiring the view through the floor-to-ceiling windows revealing half of Manhattan.

Avril returned to the living room, this time wearing a frilly little apron. My heart rate picked up, just thinking of what I wanted to do to her in that thing.

"Do you think you'll get to keep this place?" Ash asked.

She joined us, sinking into a plushy chair. "That remains to be seen. A lot of things remain to be seen," she said, staring into her flute of something bubbly.

"What's this about your selling the gallery?" Chase asked.

So he'd heard too. I guess with a group like ours, word traveled fast. Just as well. We didn't need to be keeping secrets from each other.

"Let me get everyone to the table first. We'll talk over dinner."

Well, she didn't need to convince me to come to the table, with the incredible smell of meat filling her place. She served us steak *au poivre,* with some sort of pan sauce, and roasted asparagus. Christ, I thought I'd died and gone to heaven. There was at least a full five minutes where no one at the table uttered a word.

That's what you get when you feed a bunch of guys.

"To get back your question Chase, yes, I'm thinking of selling. As successful as the Kink Lab parties have been, I don't think keeping the gallery open is sustainable. The space is too large and the rent too high."

She looked around at each of us. She clearly had more to say.

"But the main reason I invited everyone here tonight was to tell you how..." her voice cracked, "grateful I am you've come into my life. It was at the perfect time, and each of you has been perfect for me in your own individual way."

Shit. What was she getting at? We were getting the heave-ho? I put my fork down. Suddenly, my filet didn't taste that great anymore.

27

AVRIL

I STOOD AT THE HEAD OF THE TABLE AND AS I SPOKE, MY four guys put down their forks and knives and looked at me.

Chase looked scared. Was he afraid of being left again? Gio looked amused. I guess nothing could faze you when your father was an arms dealer. Ash looked curious but also a bit sad. He'd just lost a good friend, and even though he'd not said much, I saw it weighing on him. And Sumner looked at me with his poker face, like a true politician's son, giving nothing away.

Of course, my voice cracked. Because it always cracked when I wanted to look like I had my shit together.

"I want you to know I feel I can only be with one of you. I hope to know soon which of you that will be. Of course, whomever I end up with has to feel the same way about me. It's hard, though. The last thing I want to do is hurt any of you."

"Now, Avril, no need to make a hasty decision—" Sumner said.

"I'm not. I've been thinking hard about this."

I didn't tell him Blu had told me the same thing—not to be hasty, and that he thought I'd be an idiot for letting any of the guys slip through my fingers.

But I had to figure out what my new life was going to look like. And it might not include the gallery, sex parties, or the four men who'd worked their way into my heart.

And it certainly wasn't going to include my ex-husband, or the bitches with Hermès bags who I'd thought had been my friends.

That night, after dinner, the guys all went their separate ways. I needed time to myself, and I think they wanted to process both what I'd said and face what had happened to their friend Smith.

They'd talked about him over dinner.

"Did anyone see him leave the party?" Sumner asked.

We all shook our heads.

Except for Chase. "You know, I'd stepped outside to call Ruby's nanny and check in. I thought I saw him walking up the street, but when I shouted after him, he didn't turn around. I just assumed it wasn't him and went back to my call," he said.

"Was it like him to not say goodbye?" I asked.

Sumner pursed his lips. "Hard to say. He was a pretty independent guy. Always had been, having grown up an only child."

"Well," Ash said, "I'd like to know more. I wonder if we could find anyone at the party who spoke to him. Or saw him."

"I'm not sure how we would do that. I mean, we're pretty careful about respecting peoples' privacy. We can't really ask people who they have and have not spoken to," Sumner said.

"Yeah, but we can ask a few of the guests we know well. If that turns up no info, then we'll drop it," Ash said.

I felt for them. I knew all too well how it hurt to lose someone close. But the worst part was, I was scared to death I was about to hurt them more.

"DARLING," Blu said, floating into the gallery with a bunch of new Barneys bags on his arms.

I hope he didn't plan on telling me what he'd done to get his latest discount. Although I was the happy beneficiary of...well, whatever he did with Juan.

We did the air kiss thing. "Make yourself at home. I need to say goodbye to my clients."

He craned his neck, always nosy. "Hey, I know those dykes," Blu said with a big smile.

Ugh.

"Would you be quiet? Act like you have some manners, please." He'd always had a big mouth on him, and he was so cute he could usually get away with it, but not when I was working.

I took down the two paintings my clients were purchasing and made arrangements to deliver them later in the week. The two women were, by any measure, *the* lesbian power couple of Manhattan and were amassing an art collection for their Hamptons home.

And I was lucky enough to know them and sell them art.

I found Blu in my office, picking through his shopping bags. "Look what I found you!" he shrieked.

I had to say, the guy had great taste. He held up a pair of wide-legged palazzo pants in a silver-grey silk charmeuse and a black silk blouse with gathers around the neck. It was stunning.

But not something I needed if I were getting rid of the gallery and my role in the Kink Lab parties.

"I like them," I said, kicking off my shoes and rubbing my sore feet. For some reason, the gallery had been unusually busy. 'Course it had been hard to run the place since my assistant Dagney had split with my husband. But what was the point of bringing in another assistant if I was closing?

"What do you mean you *like* them? You would *love* them if you had any brains. You know how much this stuff cost? And what a discount I got thanks to Juan and our—"

"STOP," I said. No need for details…

"Well," he huffed, folding everything neatly and put it back in the bags. "It's all returnable," he said with a sniff.

"C'mon, Blu. Of course I love them. They are beyond gorgeous. But I am making some changes in my life and am not sure I'll be needing clothes like this."

I reached into the bag that Blu had tried to squirrel away as punishment for my lack of enthusiasm and pulled out my would-be clothes. The silk pants did feel pretty damn heavenly. I stood and held them to my waist.

"Girl. You are gonna slay in those pants. I might even get myself a pair," he said, snatching them from my hands and holding them up to his own waist.

I plopped into my desk chair, and Blu buried our treasures back in the Barneys bags.

"So what's up with Devon?" he asked.

"We've met with lawyers, and now I'm just waiting. If not for the prenup—"

"WHAT! You signed a prenup? OHMYGOD."

Oh shit. I hadn't meant to tell him that. "Yeah. I did." I held my hand up like a STOP sign. "And I don't need to hear about it from you," I added.

I looked down at my chipped manicure. I needed to

get my act together. "He keeps digging at me about getting a car. I never knew the man I married could be so cruel."

Blu studied me. "You never drove again after Lisette was killed, did you?"

Those words still stabbed at my heart. Maybe they always would. Actually, I hoped they would. I felt like I deserved a cross to bear. Killed my sis, suffer the rest of my life.

Seemed only fair.

"You know, someday you'll stop blaming yourself. It was an accident. The same thing could have happened to you, had she been driving."

I thought back to my dream, where we'd gotten in the wreck, but she'd survived. It was like I was punishing myself, over and over, even in my sleep. I couldn't stop.

And now, this betrayal by Devon.

I couldn't get involved with Sumner, Chase, Gio, or Ash. I was a fucking mess.

"I know that intellectually," I told Blu. "But my broken heart doesn't seem to listen. And then with Smith dying..."

"I'm sorry, baby. You've been through a lot of shit."

That was all I needed to hear. The tears started streaming down my face, carrying mascara and makeup with them.

Blu ran over with a tissue.

"Ugh. Sorry," I croaked.

"Girl, how many times have I seen you cry? And how many times have you seen me? This is what besties are for." He held a tissue under my nose, and I blew.

Which struck me as really funny. "Besties are for helping you blow your nose?" I asked with a big sniffle.

Next thing I knew, I was shaking with laughter, and Blu joined me after he decided I wasn't losing my mind.

"You know it, sweetie," he said, gasping for breath as he laughed with me.

28

CHASE

WHILE WE CONTINUED TO TRY TO TALK AVRIL OUT OF abandoning Kink Lab and the gallery, we had one more party on the calendar, and she agreed to go ahead with it. It promised to be a good one.

Word had gotten out in the business community that we'd lost Smith, but no one had linked his accident to our parties. It wasn't that we had anything to hide, but it was for the best that it remained quiet. One of the biggest selling points and attractions of our gatherings was our strong security, which delivered the privacy our guests paid so dearly for.

"Hey, doll," I said, having arrived while the team was still setting up.

In her spiky heels, Avril was nearly eye-to-eye with me. I leaned in to kiss her and she returned my affection with pliant, welcoming lips. I wouldn't have minded lifting up the floaty little skirt she was wearing to let her know how hot I thought she was, but if all went according to plan, I'd have the chance later that night.

"I'm glad you're okay with hosting tonight's shindig."

"I'm happy to, Chase. I mean, I'm still thinking about what I'm going to do, but I couldn't leave you guys high and dry."

She looked around as the room was magically transformed from an austere art gallery to a sensual playroom for grownups.

"I do love Kink Lab, Chase. I really do. I just have to figure out what I'm doing with the gallery."

Her hair was twisted into a long, thick braid, something I'd hoped to grab a hold of at some point.

Down boy.

I settled into one of the sofas the movers had brought in. One of the cool things that Blu took care of for us was making sure each party was set up a little differently. The setting was always a bit of a surprise to our guests. They loved that.

"If you closed the gallery, what else would you like to do?" I asked.

Her face actually brightened. Maybe that was something she'd been giving a lot of thought to?

"Well, you know that school for special kids, where I volunteer, teaching art? I'd love to expand the program into a small center that teaches all sorts of art classes, all year round. I mean, right now, the kids get one hour a week for art. What if they had it every day?"

"Wow. That's ambitious. I'm impressed, baby."

And I was. She was always thinking. She'd suffered a big set back with her husband leaving, and she was still thinking of other people.

"On the other hand, the Kink Lab parties have brought me an entirely new clientele. This past month has been the best I've ever had. And since we're selling more, more of the top artists want me to represent them. That's a good thing. A very good thing. So I have a lot to think about," she said, sighing.

The office door blew open and Blu whooshed in. "Hey Chase." Then he turned to Avril. "Did I hear you talking about closing the gallery again, Av? You need to just quit that crazy talk, okay? You'd be lost without this place."

"Well, part of the problem is that Devon's on the lease—" she started

"Yeah, well, that bitch is goin' to prison—" Blu said, stopping himself short.

"What?" A dark frown settled over Avril's face. "What do you mean? Is he going to prison for sure, now?"

Christ. She didn't know about the extent of her ex's legal troubles? It was easy to forget that in our business community, word traveled fast. But if you were outside of it, things tended to pass by, unnoticed.

Blu sat with his mouth partly open, regret all over his face.

"Um, yeah, Av. Devon's in big trouble, sweetie. You're lucky you got out when you did."

She looked back and forth between the two of us. "Why didn't you tell me?"

I decided to let Blu answer because one, he'd known her longer, and two, I was basically a chickenshit and hadn't wanted to upset her.

"Av, sweetie, you already have so much going on. I don't think any of us wanted to upset you further."

She swallowed hard, her eyes wide.

"So he was definitely engaged in illegal activity while we were married?"

I decided to pipe in. "With all the charges filed against him, it looks like he'd been breaking the law for a long time."

"Oh my god." She dropped her head into her hands.

I reached to rub her back. I knew it hurt to deal with the shame of what someone else had done. After all, I'd been through some shit with Ruby's mother. But I also knew my girl was strong enough to hold her head high.

"C'mon," I said, taking Avril's hand. "You've been through worse, and you are not going to let this get you down."

With a deep sigh, she stood, forcing a wan smile.

Blu gave her arm a squeeze. "Yeah, Av. There's a

party out there in your gallery, and you are going to goddamn rock it."

I led her out of the office, and we dove into the party, which was getting more crowded by the minute as the guests poured in.

I waved across the room at a couple business acquaintances of mine, who nodded back discreetly. It was like the secret handshake. I might see some of these folks getting their freak on at Kink Lab, but once outside in the real world, it was like nothing had ever happened.

Avril's tension dissipated as we walked through the room—she held the crook of my elbow, smiling beautifully at our guests.

She'd clearly grown comfortable with the Kink Lab scene and nodded with approval when a beautiful woman walked past us wearing nothing more than sequined panties and high heels.

We paused to watch a couple, who I happened to know had been married for several years, enjoy each other like it was their first date. On more than one occasion, someone had told me Kink Lab had helped make their marriage stronger.

As we wandered through the party, Avril gently pulled me over to a dark corner. We ducked behind a filmy curtain, and she placed her hands on either side of my face, brushing the lightest kiss over my lips. My hand wandered up to her long braid, and she gasped when I tugged on it.

She murmured something so softly I couldn't quite make it out. I pulled back and met her gaze, head-on.

"What was that, baby? I didn't hear you."

Her eyes glittered in the dim light of the room, and I realized they were wet with tears. "I said *I love you, Chase.*"

29

AVRIL

There. I'd done it.

I'd told Chase I loved him, and before the evening was out, I was also going to tell Sumner, Ash, and Gio.

I didn't know what would become of my man-harem and the five of us, but I wanted them to know they had my love. It was the best gift I could give them.

Chase ran his fingers through his blond hair, staring back at me. My heart stopped for a moment, and I wondered if I'd told him something he didn't want to hear. If that was the case, I was prepared to deal with it. My love came with no obligations or strings attached. I didn't say those three words with the expectation of hearing them back.

Of course, it would be nice to have them returned,

but it was also nice to stand there with my handsome Chase, in a dark corner of a sexy party.

"I...uh...um," he muttered.

Shit. Had I ruined the evening?

He looked down. "I...well, I wasn't sure I would ever hear those words from you."

He touched his forehead to mine, and I closed my eyes to inhale his scent.

"I love you too, baby."

Our lips met in a furious hunger, Chase's hand slipping under my skirt, cupping the cheek of my ass. His other hand slipped down to my breast, which he teased with his flat palm.

He pulled back. "C'mon."

He grabbed my hand and directed me toward the upstairs loft. It was set up as a play area like the rest of the gallery, but frequented by few since it was out of the way. On the way up, we stepped around a woman kneeling on the stairs, pistoning her mouth over her handsome partner's cock.

Just as I passed him, he let out a growl and started bucking his hips into the woman's face. I looked back at them when I reached the top of the stairs and saw her licking him clean after what I guessed was an explosive orgasm.

I followed Chase to a silky tufted mattress in the center of the room, which was lit only by a few flickering candles.

He faced me away and bent me forward onto my

hands and knees. In seconds, my dress was pushed up over my hips and my panties were pulled down, where they hung off one ankle. My knees were parted just enough to leave my most private parts exposed to anyone who happened by.

The threat of shame and humiliation was almost more than I could take, and the excitement had me trembling.

Cool air brushed over my sex when Chase spread me open, followed by his probing tongue. He ran it from my ass to my clit, so very softly that I had to push back against his face as a way to beg for more sensation. Just when his thick fingers paused at the opening to my pussy, there was a voice in my ear.

"Baby, you know how beautiful you are?"

My eyes flew open, and I found Sumner on the mattress with me.

"Kiss me, Sumner, please," I begged.

His tongue in my mouth and Chase's in my pussy were almost more than I could take.

And then my dress was lifted the rest of the way over my head, leaving me completely naked, except for my heels.

I opened my eyes to see that Ash and Gio had joined our little party, too.

Holy shit. Was I actually messing around with FOUR guys?

Jesus, how many women got to do *that*?

"Sumner," I said.

"Yeah, baby?" he asked.

"Give me your cock. In my mouth."

With Chase still behind me, Sumner opened his trousers and pulled out his brutally thick erection, moist at the tip from his precum. All I could think of was getting that thing down my throat. I opened my mouth wide, like a hungry baby bird.

I wasn't sure what I was turning into. It didn't matter, though, because I didn't care.

I wanted all my guys, and I wanted them all at once.

I sucked the head of Sumner's cock, creating a suction that made him growl my name, releasing it, and then sucking again.

"Darling, I'm gonna fuck you, okay?" Chase said in a low voice.

I nodded as best I could with a mouthful of cock and closed my eyes to enjoy the ride.

Four pair of hands wandered over my body, tormenting my heated skin and pushing me toward a state of delirium.

Chase drove his cock inside me in one sliding motion, filling me up and nearly sending me over my edge. Someone played with my nipples, pulling and twisting them, and another hand worked my clit. I bucked against Chase to fuck him harder. I needed to come as much or more than I needed air.

And I got what I needed. He fucked me, his hands holding my hips so hard, I'd certainly have bruises later. And while he pumped me, the hands on my clit and breasts intensified the sensation. While I sucked Sumner, I reached a hand under his heavy balls and gently tugged.

I pulled him out of my mouth, just for a moment. "Oh…oh…oh…fuck me," I mumbled. "Fuck me, please."

I wasn't saying that just to Chase, but to everyone. They—all four of my guys—were making love to me at the same time, and they all brought me to an orgasm that left my head bucking and all my limbs quivering. I felt someone's hot cum squirt over my back. Sumner was back in my mouth just in time to explode there, and I knew by the way Chase held my hips and drove inside me as deeply as he could, that he was coming, too.

Holy shit.

As soon as Chase released me, I collapsed on the mattress, surrounded by my men. I held hands with someone—who, I wasn't exactly sure—and the others had their arms around whatever part of my body they were closest to.

"I have something to tell you," I started, "all of you."

"What's that, *cara?*" Gio asked.

"You okay, sweetie?" Sumner asked.

I nodded my head on someone's outstretched arm. "I love you," I said. "All of you. Sumner, Ash, and Gio."

I was surrounded by four beautiful, loving men.

"Hey, didn't you forget someone?" Ash said.

"No dude, she didn't forget me. She actually told me

first." He puffed out his chest and the other guys chuckled.

I looked at the men draped around me on the mattress.

Was this really happening? To me?

"Like I said, gentlemen, I love you all." I sat up and took the chance to meet each of their gazes.

They looked so happy. Content.

"And because I love you all," I continued, "I can't choose just one. I am just unable to. So I'm going to walk away. I won't have any of you, but then I don't have to live with the pain of having hurt any of you."

I could feel my heart breaking into a thousand pieces. I'd known what it was like to pine for someone I loved, but to feel that way for FOUR guys?

I grabbed my dress and pulled it over my head. I had no idea what happened to my panties. But it didn't matter.

30

GIO

WELL, IF THAT WASN'T THE DAMNEDEST THING.

"What the hell just happened?" Ash asked.

Sumner finished straightening his clothes and stood. "Christ, I don't know if I've ever seen anyone hightail that fast. I'm going after her."

"Wait a minute," Ash said. "Maybe she needs some time."

"I don't know. This is bullshit. She needs to know we want to share—" Sumner said.

I reached to grab my friend by the arm. "Hold on, *fratello*. Let's think this through, first. The woman needed to get away from us for a reason. Let her have a moment."

Sumner shook his head. "Look, Gio, I appreciate your European sensibility of taking things slow, but this is a woman we love. We can't let her run away without trying to stop her."

Chase held his hands up. "Hold on, Sum. I think Gio has a point. She's been through a lot. I mean, that party at the Hamptons where everyone was talking about her was only a few weeks ago. Her life's gone upside down. And then, we came along." A small smile washed over his face, and he rubbed his temples.

"He has a point, Sum," Ash added.

I turned to see Blu bounding up the stairs to the loft, his red curls flying in every direction. "I just saw Avril leaving like her pants were on fire. She didn't even say good night."

With his hands on his hips, he looked at each of us, his eyes narrowed. "What happened?" he asked, accusation written all over his face. "What did you do?"

"Blu, nothing happened. She's just conflicted."

The other guys nodded in agreement.

"It's perfectly understandable," I said.

He lowered his shoulders back to their normal position. "All right. What are you assholes going to do?" he asked with a smile. "I mean, are you gonna sit there like a bunch of idiots, or go get your girl?"

He'd always known how to handle a tense moment.

THE GUYS NOMINATED me and my 'European ways'—which asshole had said that, anyway?—to talk to the beautiful Avril. We had full respect for whatever decision she might make, and we wanted her to know that, first and foremost.

"Darling?" I asked, when she picked up my call on her cell. I was afraid she might be avoiding our calls, but it would seem luck was on my side.

"Gio," she said softly.

"*Cara,* you sound so sad. Please do not be sad because of me and the *ragazzi.*"

She sighed deeply. "I know. I just got...overwhelmed, I guess."

"Do you feel like some company? How 'bout I come over?" I asked.

"Okay. I was getting ready for bed, but I'll wait up."

Not ten minutes later, I was riding the elevator up to Avril's apartment. It was an incredible building where she lived, but I doubted she'd be staying there for much longer, with her ex on his way to prison.

Yes, that was conjecture on my part, but it wasn't looking good for the man. And that made me immensely happy.

Anyone who hurt my Avril, not to mention the hundreds of people her ex directly and indirectly stole from, would never be a friend of mine.

Avril was standing in her doorway when I turned the corner. She was beautiful in a plushy pink robe, but her eyes were red, and she had a hanky in her hand.

"My poor *bambina*. Looking at you so sad is making my heart break right in two."

She threw herself into my arms, shaking lightly as I hoped she was releasing the last of her tears.

"Come in," she said, sniffling.

I followed her to the sofa, where she sat down and put her head in her hands.

"I don't know, Gio. I don't know how I got into this mess."

"I don't see a mess. I see a *bellissima* woman who has some decisions to make about what her life should look like going forward. That's what I wanted to talk to you about."

She raised her head and looked at me. "What do you mean? What did you want to talk to me about?"

"The guys and I were talking. We have a couple things we want you to know," I said.

She gave a small laugh. "I bet you have a couple things to talk to me about. Like how I am such a bitch for getting involved with all of you."

"No, that is not true. You've got it wrong."

Her eyebrows furrowed. "What? What do I have wrong?"

I held out my hand for hers, and she grasped mine back. "I wanted to tell you two things on behalf of the four of us guys."

She nodded for me to go ahead.

"One, we all care about you very much. You know that. And our top priority is ensuring you are happy and living the best life you can. We want that for you whether we see you every day for the rest of our lives, or never see you again."

She nodded, too emotional to form words.

"The next thing is that you don't have to choose one of us. And we mean that. We are committed to sharing you. We love you and all want to share our lives with you."

She brought my hand up to her lips and pressed hard.

My heart nearly stopped while I waited for her response. I wasn't hopeful. She was a strong woman and would never be persuaded to do something she didn't want to.

"Okay."

"What was that, *cara*?"

"I say okay."

Well, English was my second language and I occasionally had trouble understanding people. So I asked again. "I'm sorry, but what do you mean by okay?"

She pushed her hair back, behind her shoulders and straightened up. With her dark eyes gazing defiantly at me, she explained. "Gio, I will be with you. I will be with all you guys. I want to make a go of it. Okay?"

"Okay!" I said.

I couldn't wait to tell the guys. But I had a woman to kiss, first.

31

AVRIL

The gallery's doorbell rang, and I ran to answer it as fast as my stiletto heels would let me.

"Hello, Avril."

I closed the door and re-locked it, turning to face my ex, Devon.

"Hi," I said, softly.

"Thank you for agreeing to see me."

It seemed he'd aged years in the few weeks since he'd been out of my life. His previously smooth skin was marred by red blotches, made all the more obvious by an ashen complexion that in the past had always in the past been tanned and healthy.

"Let's go to my office."

He lowered himself into the chair opposite mine with the sort of stiffness reserved for men thirty or forty years his senior. What the hell had happened to him?

I turned to pour us both some coffee.

"You look well, Avril," he said.

I was surprised to hear that. I'd given up my regular Pilates classes when I realized I was a pariah amongst my 'friends.' But Blu's shopping sprees had added a new, elegantly sexy component to my dressing style— one I never would have believed I'd have embraced.

There were a lot of new things in my life that I'd never anticipated.

"Thank you, Devon. How's...how's Dagney?" It still made me sick to say that name, but I couldn't bother with hating her. It was a waste of my energy.

"Oh, um, Dagney." He looked down at his hands. "She's gone..."

My hand shook, and I set my coffee down. "What do you mean, *gone?*"

"She left me. When the legal troubles heated up, she took off," he said with a bitter laugh.

The man was worse off than I'd even imagined. "Oh. Sorry to hear that."

He cleared his throat, just like he always had when he was getting to the point. "Avril, you may have heard I am probably going to prison."

He looked at me with his sad, old eyes, and I really felt for him.

"I have heard a couple things like that," I said.

He clasped and unclasped his hands, shame pouring

off him. "I'm sorry, Avril. I'm sorry for everything. I was awful to you, and I deserve everything coming to me."

Shit. What does one say to that? Should I have told him I sort of agreed, despite my pity for him? "I wish you well, Devon."

"Thank you. That's more generous than I deserve." He stood to go. "Expect to hear from my attorneys."

Was he really going there? "What? Why?" I asked.

"Whatever assets I have left after I'm charged, will go into a trust. For you."

For a moment, I couldn't say a thing because of the lump growing in my throat.

"Walk me to the door?" he asked.

I nodded and followed him stiffly.

Leaning forward, he placed a soft kiss on my cheek. "Good-bye, Avril."

He looked at me, waiting for me to say something. When my words wouldn't come, he smiled sadly, and left. The door shut behind him, literally and figuratively closing a chapter of my life.

AFTER SEEING the day's clients, I headed home.

I was fairly useless after my meeting with Devon, torn between an intense sadness for what was lost and a sick satisfaction that he was getting what he deserved. But I couldn't be happy for anyone's downfall even if they were responsible for mine. That would leave me no better than they, and I just didn't need that shit.

My cell phone's screen flashed *Sumner.*

"Hi there," I said.

"Hello, beautiful." Music was playing the background, and I heard male voices. Very familiar male voices.

"Are you with all the guys?" I asked.

"Yup. Just driving back."

"How did it go?" I asked.

"It was sad," he said.

Okay then. He didn't want to talk about it, and I got that. I'd get the story of the guys scattering Smith's ashes out in the Hamptons another time.

"Are you all coming over?"

"Yeah. We should be there in fifteen."

I called in our order to the corner Chinese restaurant.

None of us felt like cooking, and I thought it would be fun to sit around and eat out of white cartons with chopsticks. I'd had a couple six packs of Tsingtao beer delivered earlier in the day. My stomach growled in anticipation of some delicious, greasy dumplings and stir fry.

Devon never would have eaten takeout Chinese food, but I'd practically grown up on it. Funny how things came full circle.

Speaking of full circle, I'd filled two garbage bags with those ugly Hermès purses I detested so much, along with a couple Judith Leiber evening bags, and a several pair of Jimmy Choos that I'd never gotten around to wearing more than once or twice.

My darling Blu had offered to take them by the fundraising meeting that my old charity friends were holding. Those bitches were welcome to my cast-offs. I only wished I could have seen their faces when they saw all the crap I was getting rid of. I threw in a couple Burberry cashmeres to really give them the middle finger.

A half hour later, the five of us were casually sitting around my living room, eating our delicious takeout, and listening to Pearl Jam on the stereo Devon had left behind.

Where he was going, he wouldn't be needing it.

I cleared my throat to get everyone's attention. "Hey guys. I have something to say."

They paused their eating and looked up at me. Gio raised his beer and smiled encouragingly, Chase winked at me, and Ash blew me a kiss.

Good grief, those guys.

"Okay. You might know that I had a talk with Gio earlier. He expressed that maybe I didn't need to pressure myself to choose only one of you."

The looked at each other, then back at me.

"It's true, Avril," Chase said. "You don't have to choose."

"Gio said we could all stay together," I said.

Heads bobbed in agreement.

I could hardly breathe, but I forced the words, "I wanted you to know that…that I accept."

A smile slowly spread across Chase's face, quickly followed by the same for Ash, Sumner, and Gio.

"I'd like to be with you. All of you. That is, if you'll have me." My pulse pounded in my ears.

What if, after my wavering, they were no longer sure about *me*? Well, I'd just deal with it.

But as it turned out, I didn't have to worry.

They raced over to me and there were kisses and hugs all around. I could have sworn Sumner had tears in his eyes. Chase and Ash high-fived each other, and Gio grinned.

I high-fived them back, tears in my eyes, and fell into luscious kisses with the most amazing men I'd ever known.

CHAPTER 32

AVRIL

Not long after I'd committed to the guys, the DA arrested Devon.

He was only in jail, his trial a long way off, but they'd made it hard for him to get out on bail. And once he did get out, they took his passport so he couldn't flee the country. My heart broke for him, not because of what he and I could have had, but rather for how he wasted his life—everything he'd achieved and had yet to achieve. He didn't need the extra money he got from his illegal activities. He was rich before all that.

But he lost his way. Nothing was ever going to be enough. And now, he had less than nothing. He'd lost it all—friends, family, self-respect. Such a waste.

Using the trust he'd set up for me, I was able to fund

the art school I was establishing. I knew it would make him feel good, knowing his life had not been a complete waste, by ensuring special kids had access to regular art classes.

My new life was just insane, and I was insanely in love with it.

Business at the gallery was booming since I'd signed a couple of the hottest artists in the city, and the Kink Lab folks had turned out to be great patrons of the arts, too. In fact, when the gallery had shows, we were packed to the rafters, often selling out of an artist's work in one or two days. It was unheard of.

Blu had come to work for me, running the gallery *and* the Kink Lab parties so I could focus on the school.

But the best part was my new family—the four guys, and little Ruby. In fact, I'd started taking Chase's little one to work with me on occasion. She was a huge hit and great practice for what was to come.

Yep, I was pregnant.

And no, I didn't know who the father was.

Try telling that to your ob-gyn, or bringing four gorgeous men to your first ultrasound. We caused quite the sensation when we did that, but hey, we were in New York. Pretty much anything went there, anyway.

The happiest day of my life—so far, anyway—was when I sprang the news on the guys. No one was more surprised than me to see the results of peeing on that little stick, but, boy, did I shock the shit out of the guys. In a good way.

We'd been over at Chase's for a family dinner. He'd cooked a mean pot roast and we were all complaining about our stuffed bellies while hanging out in the living room with after dinner drinks.

I was holding Ruby because, well, I couldn't resist the little angel. The guys loved holding her too, but I usually got first dibs. She was so squeezable-y delicious and chubby. I never wanted to put her down. I didn't even mind changing her diapers, something I never thought I'd say.

"*Cara*, you are so beautiful with that baby. I love watching you," Gio said, sitting back on the sofa with his ankle crossed over his knee, a drink in one hand, and a big smile on his face.

Chase nodded. "You are great with her, Avril. And she's really taken to you."

As if on cue, Ruby turned and grabbed a fistful of my hair.

Chase came rushing over. "Hey, hey, Rubes, don't torment our friends." He attempted to pry her pudgy little fingers open and off my hair, but I pushed his hand away.

"I don't mind, darling. I need to get used to it, anyway."

Ash frowned. "You need to get used to having your hair pulled? By a baby?"

"She likes having her hair pulled. At least she did last night—" Sumner said.

"Okay! Let's not talk naughty in front of little Ruby. What I was trying to say…"

I looked around the room at my four loves—Chase with his blond good looks, Ash with his exotic features and coloring, Gio with his thick black hair and Roman profile, and Sumner with his dimples that made my panties wet every time he flashed them—and took a deep breath.

"I wanted to tell you guys that our little family is going to grow."

"Huh?"

"What does that mean?"

"Whatcha talkin' about, sweetheart?"

Sumner was the only one who didn't say anything.

At first, he frowned at me, like he was thinking hard. Then he tilted his head.

"Um, guys. I think I know what Avril's getting at."

"Then enlighten us, oh wise one," Chase said with a snort.

"You idiots. I think our girl is with child."

I beamed. I couldn't help it.

Gio, my emotive Italian, jumped up from the sofa and ran to me with an embrace. When he pulled away, his face was wet with tears.

Sumner sat there, nodding, and laughing.

Chase and Ash were a little slower to see the light.

The looked at each other like someone had told them the earth was flat.

And then something washed over their faces.

"HOLY SHIT," Chase hollered, running to embrace both Ruby and me. He continued, "I'm gonna be a dad AGAIN. We're all going to be dads, guys."

"I don't suppose you know who the father is, do you?" Ash asked.

"Nope, and it doesn't matter. As far as I'm concerned, this child is a gift from all of you."

The room was filled with hoots and hollers so loud they must have heard us down on the street.

Chase broke out a very special bottle of scotch. Of course, I declined, content with my seltzer water.

"You're gonna be an awesome mother, my love," Sumner said, kissing my hand.

"I hope so," I said. The sky was the limit when people believed in you like that. I only wished my sister Lisette was around to share in the good news.

Perhaps someday, the ghosts of all our pasts would slip away into distant memories. But until then, we'd hold each other up and keep learning.

We had each other, and we had love. What more could anyone need?

Did you like *The Gallery*?
Check out the next book *in the* steamy
Contemporary Reverse Harem Collection
THE COLLECTION

I hope you loved reading this book as much as I
loved writing it.
Find all Mika Lane books here:
https://mikalaneshop.com/

Dear Reader:

I'm USA TODAY bestselling romance author Mika Lane, and am OBSESSED with bringing you sassy, steamy stories with imperfect heroines and the bad-a*s dudes they bring to their knees. I'll always bring you my signature humor and heat, topped off with a modern-day happily ever after.

My first book ever was *The Day I Ate the Milkyway*, a true fourth-grade masterpiece illustrated with crayons and bound with construction paper and glue. Nowadays, steamy romance gives purpose to my days and nights as I create worlds and characters that tickle the imagination. I live in magical Northern California with my own handsome alpha dude, sometimes known as Mr. Mika Lane, and two devilish cats named Chuck and Murray.

A dual citizen of the United States and Ireland, I have on more than one occasion spent my last dollar on a plane ticket somewhere, and am always planning my next escape. I often try new recipes on unsuspecting friends, search out hiding places to read undisturbed, and sadly kill every houseplant I bring home.

I LOVE to hear from readers when I'm not dreaming up naughty tales to share. Visit my online shop https://mikalaneshop.com/ and say hello https://mikalaneshop.com/pages/meet-mika.

xoxo, Mika

www.ingramcontent.com/pod-product-compliance
Lightning Source LLC
Chambersburg PA
CBHW071243190726
48292CB00007B/2386